'An eye for an e

G000137736

Nikos gave Carrie a
tooth. I'm sure you're familiar with the biblical reference?'

He nodded with ironic amusement. 'It's only common justice, after all. What your brother did to my sister I can easily do to his.' He paused, then showed his teeth in another smile of grim anticipation. 'I'm going to make you pregnant, Miss Stevens. Gloriously and abundantly pregnant.'

Dear Reader

With the worst of winter now over, are your thoughts turning to your summer holiday? But for those months in between, why not let Mills & Boon transport you to another world? This month, there's so much to choose from—bask in the magic of Mauritius or perhaps you'd prefer Paris . . . an ideal city for lovers! Alternatively, maybe you'd enjoy a seductive Spanish hero—featured in one of our latest Euromances and sure to set every heart pounding just that little bit faster!

The Editor

Alex Ryder was born and raised in Edinburgh and is married with three sons. She took an interest in writing when, to her utter amazement, she won a national schools competition for a short essay about wild birds. She prefers writing romantic fiction because at heart she's just a big softie. She works now in close collaboration with a scruffy old one-eyed cat who sits on the desk and yawns when she doesn't get it right, but winks when she does.

Recent titles by the same author:

DARK DECEIVER

DARK AVENGER

BY

ALEX RYDER

MILLS & BOON

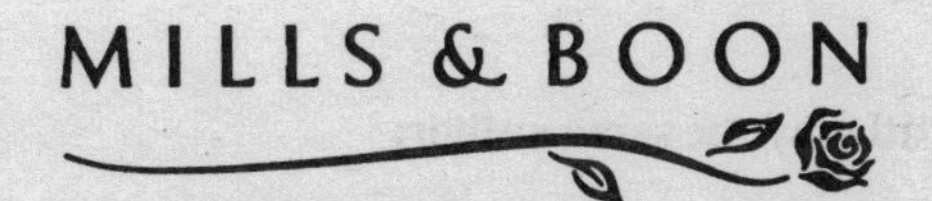

MILLS & BOON LIMITED
ETON HOUSE, 18-24 PARADISE ROAD
RICHMOND, SURREY TW9 1SR

First published in Great Britain 1994
by Mills & Boon Limited

This edition 1994

ISBN 0 263 78494 0

Set in Times Roman 11 on 12 pt.
01-9405-51040 C

Made and printed in Great Britain

CHAPTER ONE

CARRIE had pleaded, cajoled and threatened but nothing seemed to work. She gave one final frustrated push at the starter button but the ancient diesel engine refused determinedly to fire up. Swearing softly under her breath, she backed out of the cramped engine compartment and climbed on to the deck for a breath of fresh air.

She shouldn't have to be doing this, she thought angrily. Looking after the engine was Jimmy's job and he'd promised to be back an hour ago. Shading her eyes against the glare of the sun, she impatiently scanned the jetty for any sign of her young brother. She was going to chew his ears off when she got her hands on him. Her gaze took in the white-painted houses and shops facing the harbour. More than likely he was sitting in some taverna staring soulfully into the dark eyes of some young local beauty. Well, that was all very well. He was a red-blooded nineteen-year-old and he was only doing what came naturally but it was high time he remembered his responsibilities. They had a living to make. If that load of supplies wasn't delivered to the archeological team on Desvos by tonight, as promised, that would be one more customer they could kiss goodbye to.

A trickle of sweat glistened on her slender throat and ran down her neck. She wouldn't mind sitting in a taverna sipping a cool drink herself, she thought. The August heat in the Aegean could be fierce and as she looked over the side she was almost tempted to dive into the clear blue water and cool off.

The *Miranda* rocked gently beneath her feet in the slight ripples made by a boat leaving harbour and she wiped the sweat off her brow with an oily rag. They needed a new engine. No, dammit, she thought, let's not kid ourselves, Carrie Stevens. *Miranda* was getting old and she really needed a thorough overhaul and paint job, but as always it was time and money that was the problem. Financial survival depended on them providing a regular and reliable service between the smaller and more isolated islands. A thorough overhaul would take a month at least and that was long enough for some rival to step in and take over.

She looked along the jetty again, then, frowning with annoyance, she descended once more into the engine compartment.

She jabbed the starter again but the hope on her face turned to despair as the engine merely coughed instead of bursting into life as it was supposed to do.

This had happened before. Jimmy had merely grunted then grabbed a spanner and done the business and got the engine going. She should have paid more attention but she'd always had a thing about anything mechanical. A sort of mental block. Even her father, when he'd been alive, had never managed to get around that block. He'd taught her good seamanship and she knew the weather, tides and currents and how to read a chart. With a chronometer and a sextant she could navigate her way round the world if need be but the mysteries of valves, pumps and pistons were a closed book as far as she was concerned.

But things were going to have to change from now on, she told herself. They both had an equal stake in the *Miranda* and they'd have to learn each other's jobs so that in an emergency either of them could handle the boat on their own. Then again she'd had the feeling recently that Jimmy had other things on his mind. The day might well come when he'd get tired of nursing this old wreck back and forth between islands. He might very well decide to go back to England, find a nice girl and settle down, and who could blame him?

If the worst did happen she'd simply grit her teeth and carry on by herself. She certainly had no intention of ever returning to England. There were too many bitter memories for that. The *Miranda* might have seen better days but at least she provided something which Carrie had learnt to value above all else: independence. She'd tried trading that in once for the promise of a wedding-ring but Victor's promises, like everything else about him, had proved worthless.

With mounting frustration she pushed the starter a few more times. There was the usual whine then an abrupt silence which was broken by a voice from the deck. 'You're going to end up with a flat battery if you keep doing that.'

Turning her head awkwardly, she saw the tall figure silhouetted against the blue sky beyond the hatch.

She frowned in irritation at the stranger's unwarranted trespass on to her boat then thought better of it. He might be a potential customer and right now she needed all the business she could get.

Emerging on to the deck, she once more blinked in the strong sunlight and looked at the visitor apologetically. 'The engine won't...' Her voice trailed off in confusion as the impact of his appearance made itself felt.

'Won't what?' he asked in a deep masculine voice.

'Start,' she said. 'It...it won't start.' What the blazes was wrong with her? she wondered. Why was she acting like a nervous schoolgirl? Was it those eyes that were busy surveying her from top to toe?

He was tall and slim with wide shoulders and slim hips but it was definitely those eyes that held her attention. Light jade-green eyes, all the more startling in someone with the dark complexion of the southern Mediterranean. He was wearing dark trousers and a crisp, blinding white shirt unbuttoned down the front to reveal the hard muscles of his chest rippling beneath the smooth sun-darkened skin. An expensive gold Rolex watch gleamed dully on his wrist and his shoes were handmade Italian unless she was mistaken.

She felt her insides curling in embarrassment. If he was a potential customer she shuddered to think what kind of impression he was getting. An old converted fishing boat with peeling paint, sun-bleached woodwork and a dodgy engine was bad enough but her own dishevelled appearance wasn't likely to inspire confidence either. Her unkempt blonde hair was crammed beneath a grease-stained baseball cap. Jimmy's overalls hung round her like a hobo's tent and her face was streaked with oil.

The green eyes appraised her briefly, took in the state of the littered deck then returned to fasten on her once more. After a nerve-racking silence he spoke sharply. 'I'm looking for Miss Stevens, the owner of this... this floating junkyard. Where is she?'

His derogatory tone and description of *Miranda* annoyed her but she swallowed her pride. When times were bad it was something you quickly grew used to.

'I'm Carrie Stevens,' she said with quiet dignity. She made an embarrassed gesture towards the engine compartment. 'It's nothing serious. My brother will be here any minute now. He'll fix it.'

His eyes widened a fraction and he looked disappointed. 'You're the older sister of James Stevens?'

There always came a point where you couldn't swallow any more pride and this was it. Just who did this character think he was, talking down to her like that? And what did he have to do with Jimmy? Jimmy had never ever mentioned meeting a tall, dark stranger with green eyes and a built-in sneer.

She drew herself erect and challenged him frostily. 'Just what is it that you want to see me about, Mr—er——?'

'You'll find out all in good time,' he informed her coldly. 'May I suggest that you change into something more befitting a woman, and wash the grime off your face? Only then will I answer your question.'

Under the oil her face reddened and she said resentfully, 'Look, I... I didn't expect anyone. We're due to sail now. Anyway, how I care to dress is my business and no one else's.'

He ignored her outburst and went over to the engine compartment. Glancing in, he shook his head in wonder then turned to her. 'Where did you find that? In a museum?'

She gritted her teeth and clenched her fists behind her back. 'It isn't that bad. I admit that it might be old but it's perfectly good once it gets going. Jimmy can fix it. He's done it often enough before without any trouble.'

A grim smile played across the stranger's lips. 'Ah, yes. James Stevens. Or Jimmy as you so fondly call him. Unfortunately he isn't here when you need him, is he?' He glanced at his Rolex. 'That's a pity. I was told that it was imperative that you delivered your latest cargo to Desvos by eight tonight. That's a good six-hour trip for a vessel in this condition. It has already gone two.'

'We'll make it,' she said with more defiant assurance than she felt. Damn Jimmy! If he had been here on time they'd be on their way to Desvos by now.

The stranger removed his shirt and hung it carefully on the rail. The action took her completely by surprise and she found herself staring in fascination at his tanned, lean and muscular body. Under the sunlight his skin seemed to glow like dark silk. At last she found her voice and she gulped. 'Wh—what are you doing?'

'I'm going to fix that engine,' he said curtly. 'And you, Miss Stevens, are going to go below and tidy yourself up so that I can see what you really look like.'

Her mouth opened in protest then she hurriedly closed it. There was a do-it-or-else look in those green eyes that sent a shiver of fear down her spine. This was not the kind of man you argued with, she told herself. You could tell he was used to having people jump at his command and though he had no legal right to be on board she wasn't about to discuss the finer points of the law with him. He wouldn't pay any attention in any case.

With an almighty effort she assumed an air of indifference and shrugged. 'I was just about to have a wash when you came aboard. And if tinkering with engines makes you happy then go ahead. I don't want to spoil your fun.'

Hurriedly she turned her back on him and went below, securing the hatch firmly behind her. Who the devil was he and what did he want? she wondered. People with handmade Italian shoes and Rolex watches didn't hire boats like the *Miranda*. They were more likely to go along the coast to the place owned by the Spirakis family and hire one of their gleaming motor cruisers.

She frowned. Unless... unless he was up to something shady. Like smuggling, for example! Did he look like a shady character? Yes, she decided. Very shady indeed. And dangerous. Like someone from the Greek Mafia, if there was such a thing.

Well, as soon as Jimmy got back they'd tell him that they weren't interested in anything like that and send him packing.

In her tiny cabin she stripped off, lit the Ascot in the tiny bathroom and scrubbed herself under a hot shower. Drying herself quickly, she donned a clean pair of jeans and a white cotton T-shirt then attacked her hair with a brush.

After a moment she laid down the brush and reached up for the faded picture of her father, which was pinned to the bulkhead. It had been taken shortly before he died and in the picture he was standing on the deck of the *Miranda*, grinning and looking indestructible. Any time she felt disheartened and ready to pack it all in she just had to look at this picture and it made her feel better, stronger and ready to fight for what was hers and Jimmy's.

The *Miranda* had been her father's pride and joy. An ex-navy man, he'd always dreamed of owning his own boat one day but marriage had put that dream on hold. When her mother had been alive he'd worked industriously in a nine-to-four office job, hating it but never complaining.

She'd been twelve and Jimmy had only been six when their mother had been killed. Just out shopping, for heaven's sake! One minute strolling home from Tesco with a carrier of chicken breasts and cold ham and in an instant her life taken by some drunken fool of a company director driving home after a boozy lunch.

It had left them all shattered. But the agony hadn't ended there. The driver had got off with a five-hundred-pound fine and two years' suspension. There was justice for you! She'd often wondered since then if the driver and the judge had been members of the same old boys' club. Probably. It was a lousy world and these things happened.

The compensation paid by the driver's insurance company had been equally derisory and in disgust her father had suddenly whisked her and Jimmy off to Greece. Later he'd told her that there had been too many memories of her mother and he could never face the thought of spending the rest of his life in an office.

He'd found *Miranda*, drowsing and neglected at a quayside in a place called Kiparissia. She was a converted sixty-foot fishing boat and they'd all fallen in love with her at first sight. Her father had found the owner and completed the deal that very day and two days later they had headed south round Cape Matapán then east into the Aegean with its thousands of islands scattered like green emeralds across the vast blue shimmering sea.

For two months her father had been content to sail whenever the spirit moved him. Somewhere at the back of his mind he must have been wondering how they were going to live when the money ran out but he was content to leave that in the hands of fate, and it so happened that fate duly obliged.

One afternoon they had dropped anchor in a secluded bay on a tiny island when they were hailed frantically from the shore by a man waving a handkerchief. Her father had rowed ashore in the dinghy to see what was the matter and had duly returned with the news that he'd been hired to transport a wedding party of fifteen to the next island.

It seemed that the owner of the boat which was supposed to have taken them had celebrated too freely the previous night and was still out of combat.

They'd no sooner done that job than a guest at the wedding hired them to transport a dozen sheep to the nearest market.

By word of mouth their business had grown. The larger islands were served by the regular ferry lines but the smaller and more remote communities were badly in need of such a service as the *Miranda* could provide.

It had been the most wonderful two years of her life but it couldn't last. Their father had rightly enough decided that their education was being sadly neglected and, much to their dismay and his sorrow, he'd sent them back to separate boarding-schools in England.

After the free and easy life aboard the *Miranda* the rigours and discipline of a strict school had been like a douche of cold water, but looking back on it now she knew that it had been a valuable experience.

Greece of course was only a few hours away by plane and every school holiday had found her and Jimmy flying out to spend another few glorious weeks with their father.

Then she'd made the biggest mistake of her life. Even now, seven years later, she still felt sick at heart when she thought about it. She'd been eighteen, and with her father's approval she'd decided to stay in England and go to university, but she'd never even got as far as applying for a place. Oh, no. Trust her to make a mess of everything.

She pinned the picture of her father back on the bulkhead then stared at herself in the mirror. No. She wasn't going to think about Victor. That was all in the past. It was history and she had no desire to re-open old wounds.

Hurt and bewildered at the time, her first thought had been to rejoin her father but she'd had second thoughts. For one thing, Jimmy had still been at school and it might have seemed to him that he was being deserted and forgotten. But there had also been a darker and deeper reason—guilt and a feeling of self-disgust. A failed relationship surely didn't mean that she herself was a failure, did it? The only way to find out was to stay and try to make it on her own.

She'd enrolled in a college for a two-year course in business studies, then, armed with her diploma, she'd set out, brimming with confidence, to land a job worthy of her talents.

Well, there were jobs in plenty. Part-time check-out operator. Part-time barmaid or waitress. Girls with better qualifications than she had were cleaning offices to earn a living.

Things would get better once the recession was over, they kept telling her. She'd eventually landed a job with a travel agency where her knowledge of the Greek islands and proved a great asset, but the sight of all those tempting travel brochures had only unsettled her and made her long once more for the feel of a deck beneath her feet. Nevertheless she had stuck it out.

It was two years later when her father had died in a sudden and tragic accident. Jimmy had left school by now and had started an apprenticeship in a local garage. They had both flown out in time for the funeral and found comfort in each other's arms at this time of the greatest grief they had ever known.

When the service was over they had both shaken hands with the many friends who'd come to pay their last respects, then their father's lawyer had driven them to his office.

There was a little money, he had explained, but if they were interested he could dispose of the *Miranda* for them. He was sure he could find a buyer prepared to pay a reasonable price.

'No!' She and Jimmy had turned down the offer in unison and they had looked at each other in mutual understanding. The *Miranda* had been their father's dream and to sell it to a stranger would be an insult to his memory. Besides, England no longer held anything for them. They'd keep the *Miranda* and carry on the business their father had started.

The lawyer had looked at them doubtfully but when she had assured him that she and Jimmy could easily handle the *Miranda* between them he'd reluctantly given in and agreed to see to the necessary formalities and paperwork.

Three days later, full of confidence and with a list of their father's regular calls, they had set off in the Miranda to deliver a load of piping and a water pump destined to make life easier for the villagers on a tiny island south of Naxos...

The faint noise broke into her thoughts and she felt the slight tremor as the engine began throbbing. Good. Jimmy must have returned. Now she could tell that interfering stranger to go away and mind his own business.

Her blue eyes stared back at her critically from the mirror. The years in the sun had bleached her naturally blonde hair to platinum. Usually, for practical reasons, she kept it short, but she hadn't been near a hairdresser for months. Now she simply tied it back carelessly with a black ribbon. She never wore make-up, not even on the rare occasions when they found themselves calling at one of the larger islands during the tourist season. Her complexion and colouring were entirely due to her active outdoor way of life. No cosmetic had yet been made that could compete against sunshine and soft rain.

Finally she slipped her feet into a pair of rope-soled sandals and made her way up on deck.

Emerging into the daylight, she stood for a moment frozen in surprise, then she gasped in outrage. Not only had the stranger managed to start the engine, he'd also cast off the bow and stern lines and was now in the wheelhouse, and they were already a hundred yards away from the jetty and heading out to the open sea!

Frantically she gazed around the deck and into the engine compartment but there was no sign of her brother. Furiously she called up to the wheelhouse, 'Hey! You there! What the hell do you think you're doing? Turn this boat round immediately.'

The stranger ignored her for a few moments while he consulted the compass reading then he locked the wheel and casually descended to the deck to confront her.

He still wasn't wearing his damn shirt, she noted with discomfort, and she glared at him. 'Turn this boat round. My brother isn't here yet.'

The green eyes were now roving over her body with an intense interest and the raising of a dark, quizzical eyebrow gave his lean features an even more devilish look. 'Surely you can't be the woman I was talking to a few minutes ago?' he drawled. 'She was shapeless and covered in oil. You can't possibly be the Carrie Stevens I came to see. Are you?'

She felt practically naked under his hard stare of undisguised lust and her mouth went dry. 'L-look...' she stammered '...you've no right to——'

He went on as if he hadn't heard her. 'I hadn't expected anyone quite so sexually attractive, Miss Stevens. But the fact that you are will make my mission a pleasure rather than mere duty.'

She had no idea what he was talking about but by the sound of it she was in deep trouble. Taking a deep breath, she put her hands on her hips. 'I'm going to report this act of piracy to the police. You'll be in big trouble.'

'No, you won't, Miss Stevens.' He suddenly showed a row of white teeth in a shark-like ironic smile. '"Miss Stevens" sounds far too formal. Since we're going to have a very intimate relationship I think I'll call you Carrie from now on. I am Nikos Spirakis.' He paused and for a moment his jade eyes gleamed with cold amusement. 'Does that name mean anything to you, Carrie?'

She let her eyes smoulder at him in anger for a moment then she snapped, 'No. Why should it? I've never...' She paused as a sudden thought flashed into her head. Spirakis? No, it couldn't be! And yet... There was something about him. He had that cold self-assurance that only wealth and power could bestow. She looked at him more closely then said hesitantly, 'The...the only Spirakis I've heard of is the family who own half the ships and olive groves . . .'

He raised a hand. 'I know exactly what we own. You could say that we are one of the richest and most powerful families in Greece.' There was no hint of a boast in his voice. He was merely stating a fact.

She gulped. Everyone knew about the Spirakis family but if they talked about them it was mostly in whispers behind closed doors. The general consensus seemed to be that it would be safer to spit in the devil's face than have a Spirakis as an enemy.

Of course it had all been hearsay as far as she'd been concerned but now that she was actually face to face with one she was beginning to think that there was more than a grain of truth in the accusations.

Quelling the feeling of panic that was rising in her breast, she mustered as much dignity as she could and said frostily, 'I don't care how rich or powerful you are, Mr Spirakis. You've still no right to be aboard this boat. If you don't turn us round I'll do it myself. My schedule means that I won't be back here for at least a month. I can't leave my brother stranded. At least I'll have to find out if anything has happened to him.'

His mouth gave a sardonic quirk. 'You have my personal assurance that your brother is perfectly safe and unharmed.' He paused for a moment then added softly, 'For the time being at least. His ultimate welfare is entirely in your hands.'

The colour drained from her face. 'What is that supposed to mean? Where is he?'

'Working in one of our olive groves under the strict supervision of my uncle and cousins. At least it'll give him time to contemplate the error of his ways.'

Her eyes widened and she felt a chilling knot of fear in her stomach. 'I . . . I don't know what this is all about, Mr Spirakis, but I warn you that if anything happens to Jimmy I . . . I'll——'

He dismissed her threat with a snort and his green eyes provoked and taunted her. 'You're very fond of your brother, I imagine.'

'Dammit!' she flared up at him. 'What kind of stupid question is that? Of course I'm fond of him. He's all the family I've got.'

His voice turned raw with cold condemnation. 'So you simply turn a blind eye to his promiscuous way of life because he's your brother?'

Her mouth dropped open in astonishment then she laughed uncertainly. 'Jimmy? Promiscuous? You're mad.'

'Perhaps you don't know him as well as you think you do,' he growled. 'He is an attractive youth with an easy charm. Most girls would find him irresistible. Do you expect me to believe that he hasn't exploited those assets to his advantage?'

'Jimmy isn't like that,' she said in heated defence. 'I'm not saying that he doesn't go out with girls whenever he has the chance but he would never cause any of them any . . . any harm.'

He mocked her with a derisive smile. 'Come, now. A nineteen-year-old boy isn't likely to boast of his conquests to his older sister, is he?'

That knot of fear was growing larger. She already had some idea what all this was leading up to but she prayed fervently that she was wrong.

For a moment he watched the conflicting emotions on her face then he nodded with quiet satisfaction as if he'd proved a point. Still mocking her, he said, 'It may be some comfort to you to know that your brother thinks very highly of you. He seems to worship you. At least that's the impression he gave my uncle, who had a very long and informative talk with him.'

'We've always been close,' she said stiffly.

'Good. If it had been otherwise I'd be wasting my time here.' The green eyes began stripping her again with obvious anticipation. 'Now let's talk about you for a change, shall we? Tell me about your boyfriends... your lovers. Does promiscuity run in your family?'

Her cheeks flamed and she clenched her fists. 'You can go to hell.'

He eyed her in cold silence then shrugged. 'If I go to hell then so does your brother. As I said before, his fate is entirely in your hands.'

The unmistakable note of menace in his voice sent another shiver down her back and she gulped. 'I... I've only ever had one boyfriend. It was years and years ago.'

He raised an eyebrow in frank disbelief. 'Do you take me for a fool, Miss Stevens?'

Her cheeks burned again and she gritted her teeth. 'Look, I don't give a damn whether you believe it or not. Running this ship has kept me busy. I've no time for emotional entanglements of that sort.'

'No time?' he mused. 'Or is it a case of no inclination?' The green eyes challenged her then he said softly, 'Now is as good a time as any to find out.'

She tried to jump back but he was too quick for her and she found herself suddenly imprisoned in his arms. Her cry of protest died in a gasp as he crushed her to his chest.

Grinning down at her, he murmured in approval, 'Such a soft, yielding body. Now we'll see if your lips are as yielding.' One of his hands came up to grab her hair and she found herself staring up in fear into the fathomless depths of his sea-green eyes.

She closed her own eyes quickly as his mouth descended on hers and the shock kept her rigid and tight-lipped. Undeterred by her initial refusal to respond, his tongue began teasing and probing and finally forced an entry into the warm, dark sweetness of her mouth. Oh, God, she thought. When was the last time she'd been kissed like this? When had she ever been kissed like this? This was provocation beyond endurance and she could feel her limbs losing their strength.

The warmth of his bare chest and the steady beating of his heart transmitted itself through her thin cotton T-shirt and she cursed herself for not having bothered to put on a bra. Surely he could feel her nipples hardening against his body and that would only inflame him further. The hands she raised in a half-hearted attempt to push him away betrayed her and slid under his arms to clasp his back and the touch of his smooth skin sent an aching tremor through her thighs.

As his tongue continued to explore her mouth she responded, slowly at first, then as desire swelled and swept aside reason her own tongue began replying in erotic abandon. Now every nerve-end in her body began to tingle as she felt his hand slide under her T-shirt and a low moan came from her throat as he caressed her breast. His touch was fire—a scorching heat that would brand her forever.

His knee began forcing itself between her thighs and she fought desperately to cling to the last shreds of her sanity. This had to stop. Here and now. Shocked and ashamed at the demon he'd unleashed inside her, she brought her hands round and pushed hard against his chest. Frantically she tore her mouth from his and gasped, 'Stop it! Let . . . let me go, damn you.'

Denied the pleasures of her mouth, his lips found her neck and began to trace a path of incandescent sensuality from her ear to the tender hollow of her throat. As she teetered on the brink of complete and utter surrender, wanting him, needing him to relieve this intolerable aching desire, only one tiny spark of reason shone feebly in the dark maelstrom of her mind and she raised her hands to force his face away.

With a grunt he released her and she staggered back on her heels, her chest heaving.

He touched his cheek and examined the tiny spot of blood on his finger then his lips stretched in a feral grin as he surveyed her with approval. 'So the fair English rose has a thorn. She's willing to fight to defend her honour. You've no idea how much that pleases me, Carrie.'

The scratch had been unintentional but she wasn't about to tell him that. Instead, she muttered darkly, 'If you ever touch me again I won't use a thorn. I'll use something heavy and likely to be lethal.'

He dismissed her threat with a cold, derisory smile. 'Don't worry, Miss Stevens. I've no intention of forcing myself on you again. If it were merely your body I was after you'd be pinned helplessly to the deck right now and I've no doubt that you'd be writhing in ecstasy.'

Her breathing was returning to normal and her mind was beginning to function rationally once more. Lowering her eyes, she realised that her threat had been ridiculous. She could see that now. Her puny strength was no match for that of a man of his build and power and if he'd really intended taking her against her will a mere scratch on the cheek wouldn't have stopped him. There was also the sickening realisation that he was capable of inflaming her passion to such a height. Now she felt nothing but self-disgust at her own weakness and easy arousal. Perhaps, buried deep beneath all that armour of self-discipline and moral rectitude, she really was a promiscuous little harlot at heart.

Eyeing him with resentful suspicion, she said accusingly, 'You appear to think that you've some sort of hold over me because of my brother. What did he ever do to harm you?'

'Not to me, Carrie,' he said in a voice that was suddenly harsh with bitterness and anger. 'To my sister—Helen, as you would call her in English.'

A cold hand clamped itself over her heart and she bit her lip. It was clear to her now. She knew the importance of family honour to men such as him. The idea of a practically penniless deckhand, and a foreigner at that, presuming to cast an eye on his sister must have been the ultimate insult.

'Look,' she said quietly, 'Jimmy listens to me. I . . . I'll warn him to keep away from your precious sister in future. Anyway I'm sure he meant no harm.'

The cold green eyes studied her in nerve-racking silence once more then he said bitterly, 'Helen is a beautiful girl. Eighteen years old. She was betrothed to the son of a friend. They were to be married in six months' time but thanks to your brother that wedding can no longer take place.'

'Oh, come on now,' she protested. 'Just because Jimmy went out with your sister there's no need to——'

His voice cut into her like a whip. 'He did more than just "go out" with her. He dishonoured her. She is pregnant and your brother is the father.'

The colour drained from her face and she stared at him in shocked disbelief. Finally she whispered, 'That . . . that can't be true. Jimmy wouldn't be so stupid . . . I mean . . . you couldn't be mistaken about this, could you?' As soon as she'd said it she knew that it was the kind of question only a fool would ask and she flinched at his withering reply.

'Don't take me for a fool. Did you think I'd come here unless I was absolutely certain of the facts?'

Feeling sick to the stomach, she bit her lip in frustration. How could Jimmy have been so bloody stupid? The damned idiot. It would have been bad enough had it been any other girl but he'd had to go and get himself involved with one of the Spirakis clan! Well, perhaps he hadn't known who she was and the girl had neglected to tell him. But he should have had more respect for a girl no matter who she was. She felt nothing but shame that her own brother could do such a thing.

She looked hesitantly at the mask of anger directed at her and was on the point of asking him if he was quite sure that his sister hadn't led Jimmy on then she thought better of it. He'd probably throttle her on the spot.

Adopting an air of quiet resignation, she said, 'This is as distressing to me as it is to you. I really do feel sorry for your sister. There's absolutely no excuse for what Jimmy did. He's old enough to know better. But I really don't see what I can do about it.'

'You at least agree that he should be punished?'

'What do you mean—punished?' she asked warily. She'd heard some pretty graphic descriptions of the way these proud and arrogant Greeks repaid insults to their family honour. And if the family was rich and powerful enough the guardians of the law had a habit of looking the other way.

'An eye for an eye, Miss Stevens,' he said with a grim smile, 'a tooth for a tooth. I'm sure you're familiar with the biblical reference?'

For a moment she couldn't fathom what he was talking about then a seed of suspicion exploded and bloomed sickeningly in her mind.

Seeing the effect his threat had on her, he nodded with ironic amusement. 'Yes, Miss Stevens. It's only common justice, after all. What your brother did to my sister I can easily do to his.' He paused, then, as if to make sure that she was in no doubt as to the fate he planned for her, he showed his teeth in another smile of grim anticipation. 'I'm going to make you pregnant, Miss Stevens. Gloriously and abundantly pregnant.'

For a moment her breath was taken away by the sheer callousness of the man then she glared at him with a mixture of scorn and downright anger. 'So you lied. You do intend to rape me after all. Just like the brute you really are.' She gave him a withering snort of contempt. 'You may be rich and you may think of yourself as a man of honour but as far as I'm concerned any man who'd contemplate such a thing is worth less than the scum in the gutters of Piraeus.'

It was a deliberate and calculated insult made with an outward show of bravado but the cold smile remained to taunt her.

'You've got it all wrong, my dear Carrie. I'm not going to rape you. On the contrary. You're the one who is going to make the running. You're going to plead with me to make love to you. You're going to beg me on your hands and knees.'

Uncertainty flickered in her eyes and she attempted a laugh of derision. 'You must be stark raving mad. Hell would have to freeze over before I'd do that.'

'You have a month,' he told her calmly. 'This trip will last a month and by the end of it you'd better be pregnant. Or else . . .'

'Or else what?' she demanded with a sneer.

His green eyes bored into her and he spoke every word slowly and carefully so that she was left in no doubt whatsoever. 'In that case your brother will be returned to you. But my cousins will make sure that he has neither the desire nor the ability to father any more children.'

He smiled contentedly at her look of horror then he rubbed his hands together briskly. 'Now why don't you go below and make us some coffee while I look after the boat? We've got a very interesting and exhausting month ahead of us, I should say.'

CHAPTER TWO

CARRIE stood on the makeshift wooden jetty and watched as Nikos expertly used the derrick to lift the last of the cargo from the hold and swing it ashore.

John Chambers, the man in charge of the archaeological team, checked the items against his list. 'Everything seems to be there, Carrie. You just made it on time. We were getting worried. We're down to our last gallon of paraffin and tin of beans.' He took an envelope from the pocket of his bush shirt. 'This is a list of the supplies we'll be needing by the end of September. Just the usual stuff.'

She smiled brightly. 'No problem, Mr Chambers. The *Miranda* has never let you down yet, has she?'

'Who's the new deckhand?' asked John in a loud voice, nodding in Nikos's direction.

'Just a temporary replacement,' she said in an equally loud voice. 'The more temporary the better, as far as I'm concerned.'

John guffawed. 'I suppose Jimmy is up to his usual tricks, eh, chasing the young dolly birds on Mykonos? By God, I wouldn't mind being nineteen again myself.'

It hadn't been the most tactful thing to say in Nikos's hearing and from the corner of her eye she saw him stiffen. At least now that night had fallen he'd had the decency to put on his shirt again, she noted with relief. She stood idly chatting with John while he loaded the stores into the Land Rover then she waved goodbye as he drove off then stepped over the bulwark on to *Miranda*'s deck.

Nikos had finished securing the derrick and now he glanced at his watch and grunted, 'We can be on Paraxis within an hour. Cast off the lines and I'll start the main engine.'

She glared at him and said stiffly, 'This is still my boat. I'm not taking orders from you. Tomorrow we're heading south. Paraxis is in the other direction.'

'I need to buy some clothes,' he said sharply. 'I've nothing but the things I'm wearing.'

'That's not my fault,' she retorted. 'You should have thought of that before you took it on yourself to——' Her sentence ended in a squeal as he grabbed her and unceremoniously lifted her up and dumped her back on the jetty.

'Have it your own way,' he growled. 'You can stay here tonight. I'll be back to pick you up in the morning.'

Furiously she watched as he turned his back on her and ducked into the engine compartment. His head reappeared for a moment and he shouted, 'You can spend the night with your archaeological friends. I'm sure they can find you a spare tent.'

If only she could, she thought bitterly. Anything would be better than having to spend the night anywhere near him but the Land Rover had gone and it would be a four-mile trek in the darkness to the excavation site. Anyway, why should she be the one to go?

Defiantly she jumped back on board and, quivering with rage, she waited to confront him. If only some fairy godmother would turn her into a man for five minutes. A great hulking brute of a man with no neck and tattooed knuckles. Two minutes would be enough. That would give her enough time to teach Nikos Spirakis a lesson he'd never forget. She'd . . . she'd . . .

The main diesel rumbled protestingly into life and Nikos emerged and grinned at her. 'So you've changed your mind? Good. Now go and cast off the stern line.'

Her voice smouldered with a low, barely contained fury. 'Let's get one thing straight here and now, Mr Spirakis. No one, not even someone as high and mighty as you, will give me orders aboard my own boat. And I'd remind you of something else. The *Miranda* is not only my boat, it's my home. If anyone spends the night ashore it'll be you.'

He raised a darkly amused eyebrow. 'Your comments have been noted. Now cast off the stern line.'

'Cast it off yourself,' she snapped. 'I'm going below.'

In the privacy of her tiny, cramped cabin she sat on the edge of her bunk with her chin despondently in her hands and stared at the blank bulkhead. God, what a mess! How was it possible for her life to have been turned upside-down in so short a time? If it hadn't been for that cretin up there tonight would have been no different from countless other nights. She'd have been making dinner while Jimmy pottered about on deck, checking and doing routine maintenance. They'd have their dinner on deck then she'd wash up. Later they'd have a game of cards and share a bottle of wine and reminisce about their father and the good times they'd had. Jimmy would usually turn in first. On a warm night like this he'd fetch his sleeping-bag from below and spread it on the forecastle. She'd sit outside the wheelhouse for a while gazing contentedly at the stars until drowsiness overcame her and she too would turn in.

It had been a healthy, happy and uncomplicated way of life. They'd known they'd never make a fortune but that didn't matter. Some day Jimmy might get married—or she might meet someone and fall in love herself. Who could tell? But neither of them had worried about it. Like their late father they'd been content to leave their future in the hands of fate.

It had all turned sour now, though. Instead of being kind fate had turned out to be a mugger in a dark alley.

She still hadn't really come to terms with the ultimatum she'd been given but one thing was certain—she couldn't allow the Spirakis family to carry out their threat against her brother. It was too barabaric and horrendous to contemplate.

There was really no choice, she realised bitterly. She would have to give in to Nikos's demand. It would mean humiliation. Utter degradation. But what was that compared to being crippled for life?

Becoming pregnant and having a child she didn't want was a prospect that filled her with dismay, but how was she going to avoid it? And when she had this child, what then? She'd have to support it and look after it as best she could but how was she going to do that and continue with her carefree, nomadic way of life? The *Miranda* was no place to try and bring up an infant.

As for Jimmy, he'd have to support the girl and the child he'd so thoughtlessly fathered. His hands would be full and he'd have no time for her in spite of the fact that it was all his stupid fault.

As for Nikos Spirakis, he was nothing but a sadist. 'An eye for an eye', he'd said. But he was wrong. There was a big difference. Jimmy had presumably seduced the Spirakis girl—or for all anyone knew it might well have been the other way around—but he certainly hadn't raped her. But that was exactly what Nikos intended doing to her. He might try to deny it and twist the words but the moral blackmail he was using was simply violence on a more refined level.

The more she thought about it, the darker and more insoluble her problems became and after half an hour she gave up in disgust and went up on deck to cool off.

Her abductor's face was a mask of shadow and light as he glanced down at her from the dimly lit wheelhouse and she turned her back on him disdainfully and stared ahead. The starlight reflected from the still and silent sea and dead ahead she could see the brighter lights of Paraxis.

The *Miranda* seemed to be moving faster than usual and she scowled. That meant that the throttle was wide open, which meant more engine wear and higher fuel consumption, but of course he wouldn't let a little thing like that bother him. Glancing aft, she noted the phosphorescent wake stretching backwards, true and straight, and she grudgingly had to admit that, apart from the engine, he certainly knew how to handle a boat—but considering that his family was big in the shipping business that was hardly surprising.

Soon she could hear the sounds of the island carrying faintly across the water—taxi horns and the steady thump from one of the discos. She had no time for the larger Greek islands during the tourist season. It seemed to her that the main seafront towns and villages tarted themselves up like good-time girls out to make a fortune while the pickings were good. They made her feel sorry and ashamed for the inherently decent islanders.

However, that was their worry. She had enough of her own to think about.

Suddenly her heart was in her mouth as Nikos took the *Miranda* at full speed into the crowded harbour. He headed directly towards a vacant berth at the quayside, threw the engine into reverse at the last moment, spun the wheel and nestled the *Miranda* gently alongside. She let out her breath in a sigh of relief. Damn him! He'd just done that to frighten or impress her.

Standing resolutely with her arms folded, she left him to do the tying up. As soon as he was ashore she was going to go below again, have some supper then lock her cabin door and try to get some sleep.

Nikos had other ideas. Grabbing her by the waist, he practically lifted her off her feet as he pulled her on to the quay.

Pushing him away, she spat, 'Let me go. I'm not going anywhere with you.'

The green eyes glittered dangerously for a moment then he relaxed and smiled coldly. 'You've no option, Carrie. If I leave you alone you might decide to do something stupid like sailing off without me. Of course I'd catch up with you sooner or later but in the meantime I'm afraid that your unfortunate brother...' He shrugged and left the sentence unfinished.

The anger in her eyes turned to bitter defeat and she muttered savagely, 'All right! I give you my promise not to leave the harbour. Does that satisfy you?'

He contemplated her calmly for a moment then shook his head. 'I don't know yet whether you're trustworthy or not. I'll find out in time but until then I prefer to keep an eye on you.'

There had to be some sophisticatedly cutting reply to that but she couldn't think of it. Finally her shoulders slumped in obvious surrender and he nodded in satisfaction. 'That's better. First I'm going to arrange for a change of clothes and other essentials. Then we're going to enjoy a meal and a few drinks like any other normal and friendly couple. Now why don't you cheer up and make the best of it?'

She looked at him with wrathful indignation and gritted, 'I'll make the best of it but don't ever get the idea that I could conceivably enjoy your company.'

He tilted her chin upwards with his forefinger and grinned. 'You can at least pretend, can't you? After all, you're going to have to do it sooner or later.'

The street along the seafront was a bedlam of noise with loud music blaring from speakers hung outside tavernas and nightclubs.

Ignoring the cheaper eating establishments, he led her to a quieter part of town and presently she found herself being ushered through the impressive foyer of a rather de luxe hotel and unerringly steered towards the room marked 'gourmet restaurant'. She noted the white linen tablecloths and the gleaming silver.

They had barely entered when a large, rotund man with enormous whiskers issued from a side-door and greeted Nikos warmly. Like two long-lost brothers they spoke to each other in a torrent of Greek until Nikos paused and took the trouble to introduce her. 'Stavros, this is Miss Stevens. She also is in the shipping business.' He eyed her with cool amusement then added, 'At the moment we're discussing a merger.'

The sarcasm was meant for her and not the owner, who gave her a comical little bow. 'It is my pleasure to meet you, Miss Stevens. Nikos and I have been friends for a long time.'

She smiled back politely. Any friend of Nikos Spirakis was no friend of hers but she wasn't going to make a case out of it. The evening was going to be difficult enough as it was.

Stavros led them to a secluded table then gave a signal to a hovering waiter who came over smartly with a bottle of wine and two glasses.

Nikos examined the bottle and raised an eyebrow. 'Cava Clauss! How did you manage to get hold of this?'

The owner beamed with pleasure at the reaction and he spread his hands. 'With great difficulty, Nikos. I keep a special stock of it for friends such as yourself.'

Nikos handed it back to the waiter who obligingly filled two glasses. Carrie lifted hers reluctantly and took a sip. She usually prefered white to red but this was surprisingly good, dry and very full-bodied. She took another, larger sip, then, realising that the owner was watching her with anxiety, she laid down her glass and said, 'I like it.'

His face split into another grin and he turned to Nikos. 'Miss Stevens has excellent taste. Perhaps she would like to order now?'

Nikos handed her the menu but she ignored it. 'I'd like *souvlaki* if you have it.'

'And I'll have the same,' said Nikos. 'But first I'd like a pen and some paper, Stavros.'

With a snap of his fingers Stavros sent the waiter scurrying off to fetch the requirements and when he'd returned Nikos scribbled down a page of instructions and handed them to Stavros. 'Can you take care of all this for me, old friend?'

Stavros read the list then grinned. 'No problem. Everything will be taken care of to your satisfaction.'

When he'd gone she looked across the table suspiciously. 'What was all that about?'

'A shopping list,' he answered casually. 'Now, sit back and relax and enjoy your wine.'

Relax? Now there was a laugh for you. She helped herself to another sip then took in her surroundings with grudging approval. On the few occasions when she and Jimmy found time to dine ashore it was usually in some cheap and cheerful taverna. This place looked as if they charged an arm and a leg—not that that would matter to a Spirakis. He probably had shares in the place.

At the moment he seemed content just to sit there, drinking his wine and watching her under those dark, brooding brows of his. She tried her best to ignore him and spent half the time staring over his head and the other half examining the pattern on the carpet.

When the meal arrived it at least gave her the chance to concentrate on something else. She shouldn't have felt the least bit hungry. Stress and anger had being doing terrible things to her digestion but quite suddenly her appetite came back. Perhaps it was the wine or the delicious smell of the spit-roasted lamb and the well presented salad. Anyway... at least he was paying for it.

When they'd finished and the plates had been removed he refilled the wine glasses. She'd already had two with her meal and that was normally her limit but what the hell. Her situation as of now could hardly be described as normal. She'd never been drunk in her life but perhaps this was the time.

She was too preoccupied with her own thoughts to hear what he'd said at first and it was only the mention of the *Miranda* that caught her attention. 'What about the *Miranda*?' she asked sharply.

'I was saying that in spite of her looks she's a fine craft,' he repeated patiently. 'She's not Greek-built. How did you come by her?'

She'd had no intention of indulging in any kind of conversation with him if she could help it but he'd hit right on her weak spot.

'She was my father's,' she told him. 'After he died Jimmy and I took her over. And you're right. She's not Greek. She was originally a seine netter built in Scotland to withstand the rigours of the

North Sea. She can handle anything the Aegean throws at her.'

She saw the amused tilt of disbelief on his brows and she felt irritated. Well, if he intended staying with her for the next month there was a good chance they'd be caught at sea by the Meltemi, the vicious wind that struck suddenly from the north. Then with any luck he'd turn green and spend his time retching over the side. Or was that too much to hope for?

'Tell me about your father. What kind of man was he?'

Damn him. That was another of her weak spots.

Somehow the evening wore on. Another bottle of wine had appeared on the table and already it was half-empty and she wondered how much of the stuff you had to drink before it had any effect on you.

Eyeing her inquisitor with sullen exasperation, she said with heavy sarcasm, 'Why don't you ask me what I had for breakfast this morning? You've asked just about everything else.'

'Not quite,' he said suavely. 'Tell me about this ex-boyfriend of yours. Was he a good lover?'

She blinked at him, affronted at his sheer cheek. 'That's none of your damned business,' she snapped angrily.

His voice growled across the table at her, low and threatening, 'I'm making it my business. So tell me.'

Undaunted, she glared right back at him. 'I won't tell you. And there's no way you can make me.'

He merely sighed and for a moment he sat running his finger around the rim of his glass while his green eyes studied her thoughtfully, then he said,

'You still don't seem to be aware of the position you're in, Carrie, so I'll make it clear to you once more. I don't intend to spend the next month listening to your insults and looking at that scowling face. From now on you'll do exactly as you're told and you'll at least make a pretence at enjoying my company.'

'I'm not that good an actress,' she retorted bitterly. 'You're asking the impossible.'

He sighed heavily again. 'I see.' Slowly he got to his feet and looked down at her coldly. 'In that case I'll leave you. I can catch the late-night ferry and attend to your brother personally first thing in the morning. He may require a few days' hospitalisation after his "accident" but I'm sure he'll be walking about without too much discomfort in a week or so.'

Her blue eyes widened in horror at the threat and she gasped, 'For God's sake! No! You wouldn't... you couldn't...' Her voice trailed off and a voice in her head said, Oh, yes, he could. He's a damned barbarian. He wouldn't give it a second's thought.

He towered over her, waiting.

'P-please,' she stammered. 'Please sit down.'

'Only if I have your promise to behave in a more civil manner from now on.'

This was unreal, she thought dizzily. Worse than the worst nightmare she could think of.

Lowering her eyes, she bit at her lip then muttered grimly, 'You win. I... I promise.'

'That's not quite good enough, Carrie,' he said with a shake of his head. 'You're supposed to smile up at me and say, "Yes, Nikos, I promise."'

So not only did he like sticking the knife in but he enjoyed giving it a twist, she thought savagely. It looked as if she was dealing with a sadist here. She raised her eyes and almost choked over the words. 'Yes, Nikos. I . . . I promise.'

'Hmm.' He regarded her doubtfully, a faintly sardonic grin curling on his lip. 'I suppose that will have to do. It wasn't much of a smile but with a bit of practice it'll be better.' He regained his seat and folded his arms. 'Now tell me what I want to know. Was your ex-boyfriend a good lover?'

'I don't know.' She saw the gleam of anger in his eyes and she went on hurriedly, 'Look, he was the only man I've ever slept with so I wouldn't know whether he was any good or not. I mean, I wasn't keeping score or awarding points like the Eurovision Song Contest, was I?'

'Well, did you enjoy having sex with him?' he persisted.

She bridled. Perhaps he was one of those peculiar people who got their kicks from talking about intimate things like that. The retort that sprang to her lips died as she remembered her promise and his threat.

'Not particularly,' she said in quiet embarrassment.

'Then he must have been a bad lover.' He smiled at her with condescension. 'It couldn't have been your fault. Beneath your cold exterior there are raging fires of passion awaiting liberation. I felt the heat for myself this afternoon.'

Once again she flushed as she recalled the way her body had responded to his deliberate provocation. Even in bed Victor had never made her heart race out of control like that. Nikos went on with his relentless questioning, 'Is that why you left him? Because he was . . . unsatisfactory?'

'No,' she replied bitterly. 'It turned out that I was only his Saturday-night girl.'

He gave a puzzled frown. 'Saturday-night girl?'

'Yes. I found out that he had one for Monday night and another for Thursday.'

He nodded in understanding. 'He was being unfaithful?'

'You could put it like that,' she said, chancing a hint of sarcasm in her voice.

Reaching for the bottle, he refilled her glass. 'And there have been no other men since then?'

She looked at the glass. 'Are you trying to get me drunk?'

'Answer my question,' he snapped.

Simmering quietly, she replied with dignity. 'No. There haven't been any other men.' She paused then added, 'You know the old saying: once bitten, twice shy.'

The fingers of his right hand drummed a slow tattoo on the table while he thought her answer over. They were strong, very competent-looking fingers, she noted. Perfectly manicured, the half-moons translucent in light contrast to his darker skin. Finally he gave a decisive nod. 'I have the feeling that you're telling the truth, Carrie. You strike me as being open and honest.'

He'd be giving her a gold star and telling her to go to the top of the class in a minute, she thought. 'Look,' she began with a forced politeness, 'would you mind telling me why you're asking all these questions? I don't see that my previous life has anything to do with you. I mean...why should it make any difference to you what kind of sex-life I've had?'

'It matters considerably, Carrie.' His eyes measured her dispassionately. 'I wish to hurt your brother, make him suffer the same disgrace he has brought down on the heads of my family. If you were a person of loose moral behaviour, as he seems to be, he might simply shrug off your pregnancy as being of little consequence. Certainly nothing to feel disgraced about.'

The sheer cold-bloodedness of his reasoning was almost unbelievable. Recovering her breath, she looked at him with barely disguised contempt. 'I suppose it's your only regret that I'm not a virgin? That would really have made your day, wouldn't it?'

He gave a dry, philosophic shrug. 'A man can't have everything. However, I want you to know that I have nothing against you personally, Carrie. In fact, I think I'm beginning to like you. You're extremely attractive and, as I pointed out before, my mission here will be a pleasure instead of mere duty.' He spread his hands in a gesture of mock-appeal. 'Believe me when I say that I sympathise with your position but it isn't my fault that you're unfortunate enough to have a brother who doesn't share your high moral scruples.'

The rumours she'd heard about him were true, then. If this was the way he treated people whom he liked then God help his enemies.

A sudden, suspicious thought crossed her mind. At first she dismissed it as highly improbable then she decided that any chance was better than none at all. There could be no harm in calling his bluff, if that was all it was.

'I want to talk to my brother,' she said calmly.

He gave a dark frown of displeasure. 'That isn't possible.'

'Why?' she demanded. 'You said that he is being held by your cousins at some estate. I presume they have telephones there?'

He nodded. 'Of course. But talking to him will do neither of you any good. Besides, at the moment he's in an agony of suspense wondering what my plans are for you. For the moment I'd rather keep it that way.'

Once more she wondered how anyone could be so studiedly callous and in a cold voice she said, 'Well, it's like this, Mr Spirakis. You may be convinced of my honesty but I'm not entirely convinced about yours.'

His mouth tightened into a savage line of anger then he growled at her, 'You doubt the word of a Spirakis? You're treading on dangerous ground, Miss Stevens. I'd advise you to watch your step.'

'You doubted my word,' she retorted, 'then you subjected me to a humiliating cross-examination. All I'm asking you to do is allow me to speak to my brother. If you refuse then how do I know that you're telling me the truth about him—or anything else, for that matter? For all I know this whole thing could be a hoax—an elaborate scheme to put me out of business.'

'Don't be ridiculous.' He sounded bored. 'What makes you think I'd be remotely interested in an insignificant operation like yours?'

She ignored the disparaging comment and stood her ground. 'Then let me talk to Jimmy. If you really do have him then I at least have to know that he . . . that he's still in good health. Perhaps you've already taken your revenge on him and I'm just the sweet after the main course. All I've heard from you so far are accusations and threats. I want to hear the truth from his own lips.'

Again he regarded her in thoughtful silence then he shrugged. 'Very well. I'll let you talk to him briefly. If that's the only way to make you come to terms with the reality of your situation then so be it.' He signalled to the waiter.

They both sat in tense silence until the waiter returned with a phone and a long extension cord which he plugged into a socket on the nearest wall.

Lifting the handset from the cradle, Nikos pushed the numbers, waited a moment then said quietly, 'Andros? Fetch the Stevens boy. His sister wants to talk to him.'

He passed the handset across the table and she snatched at it eagerly. The instrument crackled in her ear for a few moments then she heard the breathless voice of her brother. 'Sis? Is that you?'

'Yes, Jimmy.' She paused, afraid to trust her voice, then she took a deep breath. 'Jimmy . . . are you all right?'

He sounded angry. 'Sure. I'm fine. But what about you? Is Helen's brother with you?'

She closed her eyes in relief that up to now he was unharmed.

'Sis? You still there?'

'Yes, Jimmy. And yes—her brother is here.'

'Listen, you tell him from me that if he lays one finger on you I'll . . . I'll——'

She cut him short. 'Don't worry about me. I can look after myself.' She hoped her voice sounded convincing enough.

There was an awkward pause then he said quietly, 'Look . . . I was going to tell you about Helen. You've got to believe that, Sis. As soon as I found out about her condition I was coming back to the *Miranda* to tell you but these goons just bundled me into the back of a car.'

Her heart felt heavy as lead. 'Then it's true about you and her? She's really going to have your child?'

'Yes, it's true. I'm going to be a father.' There was another embarrassed silence then he tried to make light of it. 'I guess it isn't the time to be passing around the cigars, though. Now let me talk to that brother of hers.'

A steel band seemed to be tightening around her chest and she handed the phone back to Nikos. 'He . . . he wants to talk to you.'

Nikos held the phone for a moment between finger and thumb then he dropped it carelessly back into the cradle, cutting the connection.

'You might at least have listened to what he was going to say,' she flared.

'Listen to excuses . . . pleas for mercy? It's too late for that now.' He signalled to the waiter, who came over and removed the phone.

She held her tongue as Stavros, the hotel owner, came over and grinned at Nikos. 'The accommodation you asked for is ready and the clothes you ordered have arrived.'

Nikos gave a satisfied nod. 'Good. And the other matter?'

'It is being attended to. The men say it will take a few hours. It will be ready in time and you will have no cause for complaint. They are the best on the island.'

Most of the conversation had been above her head but one item had caught her attention by the throat. He'd ordered 'accommodation'!

As soon as Stavros was out of earshot she hissed across the table, 'I'm not staying here. I'm going back to the boat.'

'I'm afraid that won't be possible,' he drawled. 'But you needn't worry. The rooms are separate.'

'With a connecting door, I've no doubt,' she ventured bitterly.

'No.' His teeth flashed again in that predatory smile. 'I dare say that you're now impatient to get the whole thing over with as quickly as possible but tonight wouldn't be a good time to start. You've had a very trying day and you're tired. I'd rather wait until you're fully recovered from the shock. After all, I want you to enjoy the experience as much as I know I shall.'

CHAPTER THREE

BY MID-MORNING they were halfway to their next port of call and Nikos studied the chart then glanced at his watch. 'We should be there in a couple of hours. What's the cargo this time?'

'Won't know till I get there,' she answered coolly. 'Perhaps vegetables to take to the nearest market.' She swept her blonde hair off her face. 'Anyway we're calling somewhere else first.' She kept the wheel steady and stared fixedly over the blue silk sea. Well ahead of them a 'flying dolphin', one of the large hydrofoil ferry boats which served the larger islands, crossed their bows on its way to Samos.

'Where?' he demanded in mild irritation.

Glad of the chance to show that she was at least in charge of the boat if nothing else, she snapped, 'That's my business. You'll find out when you get there.'

Like her he was wearing jeans and rope-soled sandals but again he was stripped to the waist and in the confined space of the wheelhouse occasional contact was inevitable. He did it again—his bare chest brushing against her equally bare upper arm—and the electric tingle made her nerves jump. He was probably doing it deliberately, she decided. She was quite capable of steering in the right direction and there was no need for him to lean over and consult the compass every two minutes.

With a betraying tremor in her voice she said, 'Look, Nikos... there isn't room in here for both of us. Why don't you go out on deck and... and find something else to do?'

His eyes held a green flicker of amusement at her apparent discomfort. 'We're going to be a lot closer than this, Carrie. I thought you'd have been used to the idea by now. However, if my nearness is disturbing you then you can leave the wheel to me. You can go below and make some coffee.'

Averting her eyes, she squeezed past him with difficulty and made her way down to the tiny galley.

The headache she'd woken up with this morning was still fighting a rearguard action against the aspirin and orange juice which was all she'd felt fit to face at breakfast.

Nikos, wolfing into an enormous helping of yoghurt and honey, had eyed her across the restaurant table with a touch of concern, though whether it had been genuine or not she still wasn't quite sure. 'No appetite? Didn't you sleep well?'

She'd just looked at him in brief, bitter silence, not bothering to answer.

He'd shrugged. 'Never mind. The sea air will clear your head.'

They'd left the hotel shortly afterwards. Carrying the new holdall containing the clothes he'd bought, he had led the way along the already busy seafront towards the harbour and on board the *Miranda*.

As soon as he had stepped on deck he had tossed the holdall aside and peered into the engine compartment, then gestured her over. 'That's why I didn't want you to return aboard last night. The noise of the mechanics working would have definitely kept you awake.'

She gazed into the engine compartment and her blue eyes widened in astonishment. 'Th-that's a brand-new engine! Wh-where did that come from?'

'Maybe the tooth fairy brought it?' His sardonic comment turned to a low growl. 'I ordered it to be installed last night.'

'You had no right,' she spluttered. 'I can't afford to pay for a new engine! The old one could have been reconditioned.'

'No one is asking you to pay for it,' he said sharply. 'If I'm going to spend a month on this thing I don't want to be caught in a storm with an engine that's ready to expire of old age.'

There was a thick book in a clear plastic cover lying on top of the engine and he tossed it carelessly at her. 'That's the maintenance manual. It's painfully obvious that you know nothing about engines so I advise you to study it carefully in your spare time.'

'Spare time?' She looked at him resentfully. 'I'm going to be too busy trying to preserve my dignity to have any time to spare.'

'I wouldn't put too high a price on my dignity if I were you,' he said grimly. 'I don't think your brother would appreciate it.'

There it was again, she thought with despair. The threat. The dark reminder.

She had looked at the engine again, grey, squat and very powerful-looking. And expensive. A year's pay would hardly have covered the cost and yet he was virtually giving it to her as a gift! Could it be that his conscience was troubling him and this was his way of...of...? No. She had dismissed the thought. Proud and arrogant men like him never suffered from pangs of guilt. More than likely he was simply worried about his own skin if there really was a storm.

Five minutes later the *Miranda*, her new heart beating with a strong regular rhythm, had left the harbour and headed eagerly for the open sea.

When she took the coffee to the wheelhouse he accepted it with a grunt of thanks then gestured ahead to the smudge on the horizon. 'There's Skiati.'

'Steer five points to port,' she told him. 'There's a tiny island just north of Skiati. We're calling there first.'

He eased the wheel over and brought the *Miranda*'s bows round to the new course she'd given him. Standing behind him, she smiled in grim anticipation. When he'd taken it upon himself to sail with her and take Jimmy's place he hadn't really known what he was letting himself in for. Well, he was about to find out the hard way.

The sun was almost overhead when they anchored in the tiny bay and the heat from the *Miranda*'s deck rose in shimmering waves. It was not much cooler as they rowed the dinghy towards the beach.

When Nikos dragged the dinghy up on the sand he surveyed the scene before him and looked at her quizzically. 'Now what?'

Inland from the beach there was nothing but bare scrub stretching for two hundred yards before it began to rise steeply and she pointed up the hill.

'We're going up there to meet an old friend of mine.'

Without any further explanation she marched up the beach and began picking her way cautiously along a narrow path leading through the scrub. There was no guarantee that he'd follow. He might decide to laze on the beach or go swimming until she returned, but she doubted it. Curiosity, if nothing else, would compel him to find out what she was up to. After a moment she heard the rustle of the scrub behind her and she smiled in satisfaction.

In the heat it was exhausting work climbing up the steep hill and she was glad when it finally and suddenly levelled out. This place had been invisible from the beach but now they were walking through about four acres of patchy fieldwork towards a crumbling white-painted house.

When she was near enough the house to be heard she called out, 'Kati?'

At her second call a figure in a black shawl appeared at the doorway and raised an arm in greeting.

'Who is she?' asked Nikos.

'She lives here on her own,' she explained quietly. 'She's nearly seventy. A widow.'

'No family?'

'They left here long ago for a better way of life. Kati refuses to leave. Her husband is buried here.'

'It can't be an easy life for her here on her own,' he observed. 'She's a foolish old woman not to join her family.'

'I just told you that her husband is buried here, didn't I?' she retorted. 'To some people in this world a thing like that is important. I'd probably do exactly the same.' She eyed him bitterly then went on, 'Anyway, I've never heard her complaining. She grows all her own food and she has a few sheep and goats. Now and then her family send her a little money. Her real problem is fresh water. The well up here ran dry years ago. Now the only well on the island is at the foot of that hill we just climbed.'

They were drawing closer to the house now and she lowered her voice. 'She's a very determined and independent old lady and she can manage most things on her own. What she can't manage is carrying ten gallons of water at a time up that hill.' She shot him a meaningful look. 'Jimmy and I always make a point of calling on her at least every six weeks. In exchange for some of her goat's-milk cheese Jimmy always offers to top up her storage tank with fresh water from the well. Sometimes it takes him a couple of hours. It depends on how dry it has been and how much she has used.'

Nikos, still looking cool and not the least out of breath after the climb, grunted. 'You brother must be extremely fond of goat's-milk cheese.'

'He isn't. He hates the stuff.'

The green eyes narrowed and he smiled thinly. 'I see. So that's why I'm here. To be a water carrier. How large is this water tank?'

'Two hundred gallons,' she said calmly. 'At ten gallons a time that means twenty trips to the well.' She gave him a taunting look from her blue eyes. 'Of course, you may feel it's beneath the dignity of a man like yourself. Or perhaps you aren't as fit as you look. I suppose you spend most of the time in an air-conditioned office lifting nothing heavier than a telephone. A man with nicely manicured nails like yours won't be used to really hard work. I suppose I'll end up having to do it myself. It'll take a lot longer but I can't leave old Kati to do it herself. I'll just tell her that——'

He interrupted her with a loud snort of impatience. 'For pity's sake stop your yammering, woman. I'll fill her damn tank.'

She smiled coldly. 'Good. I was hoping you'd say that.'

He didn't waste any time, she noted with satisfaction. As soon as she'd introduced him briefly to Kati he took the two plastic containers and disappeared down the hill.

Kati was disappointed that Jimmy hadn't come but she spun the old woman a yarn about Jimmy having gone to England for a few weeks.

Then Kati's eyes twinkled. 'And this man Nikos? He is very handsome. It is about time you had a man like him. He looks strong, just like a good husband and father should be.'

She managed to get off that subject quickly enough and now she was helping the old woman to bake some bread in the wood-fuelled outdoor oven. The sun beat relentlessly down on her back and when the bread was made both she and Kati sat in the shade near the front door.

They stopped chatting for a moment and watched as Nikos appeared at the top of the path and made his way towards the water tank with a full five-gallon container in each hand. As he drew nearer she saw the way the corded muscles of his arms, shoulders and stomach were ridged with tension.

His mahogany-coloured chest was glistening and he'd tied a rag around his forehead to prevent the sweat from his brow stinging his eyes.

Kati clucked in sympathy. 'He has carried enough. The tank must be over half-full by now. That's all I'll need. Call him over and we'll have a glass of wine.'

Carrie gave a light, dismissive laugh. 'Let's just leave him to carry on, Kati. Nikos enjoys hard work. He'd never forgive me if I stopped him before the job was properly done. Now, you were telling me about your daughter in Athens...'

Much later, after they'd said their farewells to Kati, Nikos led the way down to the beach in silence while Carrie followed wearing a smug little smile of satisfaction. She hoped he'd done some permanent damage to himself, or severely strained a muscle at the very least.

She placed the two fresh loaves and the slab of cheese Kati had given them into the dinghy then began to drag it down to the water's edge.

'Leave it,' Nikos said curtly. 'I need to relax for a while.'

'Why?' she asked innocently. 'Was the job too much for you after all?'

His upper body was streaked with sweat and her mocking smile froze and turned to an expression of consternation as he slowly undid the buckle of his belt. In her haste to back away she stumbled and landed on her rear end with a jarring thump. Horrified, she looked up and watched as he removed his jeans. Oh, my God, she thought. It was going to happen right here and now. He was going to take his revenge on her.

He towered over her in magnificent nakedness. In a situation like this a lady was supposed to avert her eyes and blush furiously but her eyes refused to be averted. They were staring in fascination. His thighs were thick and powerful and his . . . his . . . My God! He was big. He was. . .was. . . Her mouth was dry and she scrambled awkwardly away from him, too week in the knees to get to her feet. 'Nikos. . .? Now you keep away. . . You. . .you said that you weren't going to . . . to . . .'

'To what?' he asked sardonically. 'Have my way with you by force? Relax, Englishwoman. Surely you've seen a naked man before. I'm merely going for a swim to cool off. If you had more sense and less modesty you'd do the same.'

Turning his back on her, he strolled down to the water's edge and plunged in.

It took a while for her thudding heart to calm down and shakily she got to her feet. He was right. She did need to cool off. The heat she was feeling right now wasn't entirely due to the sun. For a moment there she'd actually wanted . . . No. She pushed that disturbing thought right out of her mind, kicked it downstairs and locked it in the cellar where it belonged.

Suddenly it seemed like a good idea to go for a swim. But not here. Not this close to him. She walked along the beach to the other side of the tiny bay then glanced back. How far? A hundred yards? Well, she couldn't go any further so this would have to do. She stood biting her lip and debating with herself but finally the lure of the cool, inviting water proved too much and sitting down on the sand she quickly removed her T-shirt and bra then wriggled awkwardly out of her jeans and knickers. With a final, suspicious look across the bay she took a deep breath then stood up and took a racing dive into the water.

Blissfully she turned on her back and began a slow, leisurely backstroke. She closed her eyes and tried to relax but that thought kept hammering on the cellar door. She was going to have to do something about that man. Standing naked in front of her like that had been deliberate provocation. Oh, he was clever. Diabolically cold and calculating. No doubt about that. He'd done it to watch her reaction. And she'd fallen for it. Her eyes had lingered on him too long. Not just a fraction too long but far too long altogether, and that reaction had told him all he wanted to know.

Well, she'd just have to be a damned sight more careful in future. There had to be some way out of this situation—some way other than giving in to his impossible demand or falling victim to her own human frailty. Oh, yes, let's not forget human frailty, she told herself bitterly. Let's face up to the truth, shall we? Let's admit that he might be a swine, a bully, an egotistical chauvinist pig with a heart of ice but by God he has enough sex appeal to give a marble statue palpitations.

She wallowed about in the water for another ten minutes then made her way back to shore. Rubbing the water from her eyes, she surveyed the beach but saw no sign of him, so once again it was streaking time as she stood up and raced for her clothes.

Dressed and feeling a lot fresher, she began walking back towards the dinghy when she stopped and swore softly under her breath. His jeans were still lying where he'd dropped them, which meant that any time now he was going to emerge from the sea as naked as he'd been when he went in.

Disconsolately she sat down, her elbows on her knees and her chin cupped in her hands, and waited. When she did catch sight of him a few minutes later from the corner of her eye he was swimming powerfully towards the beach and she turned her head away.

After a while she chanced a quick look and saw thankfully that he was decent once again; she rose to her feet.

He was lying on his back with his eyes closed when she approached and, as if sensing her presence, he sat up and gave her a long, measured look. Finally he patted the sand at his side and said, 'Sit here.'

She declined the invitation hurriedly. 'No. It's time we left.'

His dark brows gathered themselves once more into a threatening scowl. 'It's time you learned to stop arguing with me. Now either you sit down voluntarily or I'll make you.'

The way those eyes of his were ripping into her was reason enough to submit meekly and she lowered herself hesitantly on to the sand.

'Not away over there,' he snorted. 'Nearer. I'm not going to eat you. I want to talk about that imbecile you have for a brother.'

She eased herself a little closer then said resentfully, 'If it's about your sister then I agree with you. But that doesn't give you the right to——'

'I'm not referring to my sister,' he snapped impatiently. 'I'm talking about his misguided attempts to help that old woman. Doesn't he realise the danger he's putting her in?'

'Kati? Danger?' A perplexed frown creased her brow. 'I don't understand what you mean. How is he putting her in danger? He's simply doing what any right-thinking person would do. He helps her whenever he can.'

'You mean he feels sorry for her?'

It sounded like an indictment coming from his lips and her frown grew deeper. 'It's not just that. There's a special kind of bond between Kati and Jimmy.'

Now it was his turn to frown. 'Bond? What kind of bond?'

It was really none of his business but a refusal to explain would only provoke his temper again. 'Well, Jimmy was only six years old when he first met Kati. My father was alive then but Jimmy missed his mother. One day we came to this island by accident—actually we were sheltering from the Meltemi in this very bay. The next morning the wind had blown itself out but Dad decided to spend a few days here. Just after breakfast Jimmy decided to go exploring. When he hadn't come back four hours later Dad and I went looking for him. We climbed the hill, saw the house and found Jimmy helping Kati to milk the goats.' She paused and smiled at the recollection. 'To cut a long story short Kati and Jimmy took to each other straight away. Kati was missing her family and Jimmy needed a mother so they found in each other the things they wanted most.' She shrugged. 'It's been like that ever since. As I said, we always visit her as often as we can manage.'

'Very touching,' Nikos said drily. 'And what would happen to her if she fell ill while you weren't here? At her age she could easily fall and break a brittle bone. She should be with her own family where she belongs.'

Puzzled by his reaction, she said defensively, 'We know that. But if her own family can't persuade her to leave what chance have we got?'

'You can stop filling her water tank for her for a start,' he responded harshly. 'You and your brother are only making it easier for her to defy the wishes of her own children. If your brother was more interested in her welfare than in playing the part of a surrogate son he'd do everything in his power to make her leave. By force if necessary.'

'But . . . but her husband is buried here. She says she couldn't leave him.'

'An old woman's foolishness,' he said dismissively. 'Her husband's grave will always be here. There's nothing to prevent her coming back to visit any time she likes. It's certainly no reason for incarcerating herself on a place like this.'

She stared at him in bleak and angry silence. He was quite right, of course. What he said was true. It was the only sensible thing to do. It was also the cold and callous solution she might have expected from a man like him.

Her despair deepened as a new thought occurred to her and she voiced it bitterly. 'Since Jimmy won't be coming back I suppose that Kati will have no option now but to leave. I suppose I should go up there now and break the news gently. In a couple of weeks' time, when she's got used to the idea, I'll come back and take her to the mainland.'

Another one of those dark frowns settled on his face and she braced herself for another tongue-lashing. Nothing she said ever seemed to please this cretin. 'Why do you say that your brother won't be coming back?' he asked. 'I see no reason why he shouldn't be restored to your tender ministrations in the near future. Of course, as I've already pointed out, what condition he's in depends on you.'

It was her turn to frown. 'What are you talking about? He won't come back to me. He isn't the kind of a man to run out on his responsibilities. He'll do the right thing by marrying your sister and looking after her and their child.'

He seemed to find that idea wildly amusing and he drawled, 'And who is going to look after you and your child in the meanwhile?'

She bit her lip and looked away hurriedly to hide the torment in her eyes but there was no escape from his grating laugh of derision. 'There's no question of any such marriage being allowed,' he declared coldly. 'So put your mind at rest. Our family will support and maintain your brother's child and he'll be free to maintain and support mine.'

Never had she experienced such a feeling of blistering outrage and it was all she could do to stop herself from leaping at him and clawing that cold and arrogant face to ribbons.

She waited a moment then when she was calm enough to speak without choking over the words she said, 'And what about Helen, your sister? Doesn't she have any say in the matter? Supposing she's in love with Jimmy and wants to marry him?'

'Her future has already been decided,' he asserted firmly. 'Helen will be sent to America to live with another branch of our family. When she arrives there she will be dressed in black. The story, for public consumption, is that she is a tragic young widow. In time a suitable husband will be found for her.'

She struggled to her feet and glared down at him in absolute fury. 'You...you're barbaric! Inhuman! A...a cynical, diabolical bastard!'

Slowly, inexorably he rose and towered over her. 'The only bastard in the Spirakis family is the one my sister is going to have courtesy of your brother.' The anger in his eyes turned to something more chilling and his fingers entwined themselves painfully in her hair. 'You're trying my patience again, Carrie, and I'm not a patient man. I've already warned you about your insolence. Now why don't you use all that emotional energy where it'll do you the most good? You know the rules of the game and sooner or later you'll have to make a start...'

CHAPTER FOUR

THE *Miranda*'s deck was cluttered with her latest cargo. Up on the foredeck there were a dozen stone jars of olive oil, four crates of chickens, two goats, a lashed-down upright piano, various bags of fruit and vegetables and two old men sucking pipes and spitting over the side.

In the wheelhouse Carrie reached up and switched on the radio to pick up the latest weather forecast. As far as the eye could see the water was a mirror-like blue but she felt uneasy. The weather had been too good for too long and when a storm struck the Aegean it came at you like an express train.

'Why the worried look?'

She glanced round at Nikos, who'd suddenly appeared in the doorway. It had been four days since they'd had that blazing row on the beach but since then their relationship had been tolerable enough. Conversation was sparse but at least they were no longer hurling insults at each other and he'd never made any further reference to Jimmy, nor had he reminded her of the threat she was under. It could be that he was having second thoughts, relenting at last in his impossible demand, but she doubted it. Nikos Spirakis didn't strike her as the kind of man who'd ever have second thoughts about anything. If he really intended to make her pregnant nothing on earth was going to stop him. It was more likely that he was simply changing his tactics. Probably trying to be subtle for the very first time in his life.

'I've got a bad feeling about this weather,' she muttered.

He looked around at the flat, calm sea and the cloudless sky. 'What's the latest forecast?'

'Same as last time. Good weather to continue.'

He nodded. 'I see. But you've got a feeling?'

She challenged him resentfully, 'That's right! Go on. Laugh. Ridicule me. Call me an idiot.'

His features hardened and his green eyes took on that familiar hard glint. 'Do I look as if I'm laughing?'

She stared into his face then looked away in embarrassment. 'No.'

'If you say you've got a feeling then that's good enough for me,' he grunted.

Her mouth tightened with suspicion then she looked at him again, searching his face for the least hint of mockery. Finding none, she blinked at him. 'It is?'

He shrugged. 'I've had an opportunity to watch you at work over the last few days. You know how to handle this boat and you're familiar with these waters. You're a natural born seafarer and I'd trust your instinct any day.'

The unexpected compliment caught her by surprise and she felt herself colouring. 'I . . . I'm not saying that there definitely is going to be a storm,' she hedged. 'It's just that if there is then this is a bad place to be.'

'Why?' He sounded genuinely puzzled at her statement.

She explained hurriedly, 'If you look at the chart you'll see that we haven't much water under the keel. We're sailing along the top of a submerged ridge. Just north of us the sea is a lot deeper and any strong wind just creates steep rollers. In that case we'd just head into them and ride it out. But when these rollers reach the shallows they break up and the sea comes at you from all directions. Like a cauldron of boiling water, really. The *Miranda* won't sink but she'll take a hell of a pounding.'

Too late she realised that her invitation to study the chart was also an invitation to lean closer, and sure enough the smooth skin of his bare chest once again made contact with her upper arm. In spite of the tiny jolts racing through her nervous system she remained perfectly still, afraid that he might interpret the slightest movement on her part as some sort of sexual signal.

Finally, to her relief, he straightened up and grunted, 'It might be wiser to put the cargo in the hold. It's too exposed on deck.'

She nodded in agreement. 'That's exactly what I was thinking. I've never lost a cargo yet and I don't intend to start now. Even if we just get the piano and the goats in the hold for the time being it'll only take minutes to clear the rest. The two passengers can go down to the galley.'

'Right. I'll do that now.'

Switching the radio to short wave, she picked up the BBC World Service and to the strains of Mantovani covertly watched Nikos at work. Unlashing the derrick, he swung it forward and hooked it to the piano. A moment later it was in the hold and he turned his attention to the two goats. Using a piece of spare rope, he deftly fashioned a cradle and with much indignant bleating they were carefully lowered into the hold one at a time.

Well, he'd certainly gone about that in a thoroughly competent manner, she admitted to herself. Jimmy couldn't have done it quicker or better. He was obviously used to hard work. Of course she'd known from the time he'd carried all that water up the hill that he hadn't developed a body like that by lounging about in an office dictating letters.

Finally he unlashed the tarpaulin in case they had to cover the hold in a hurry.

Tearing her eyes from him, she checked the compass bearing and scolded herself as she brought the *Miranda*'s bows to the correct heading. That was what happened when you didn't keep your mind on the job you were supposed to be doing. Glancing astern, she saw the tall-tale curve of the wake drawing attention to her lack of attention at the wheel. She hoped Nikos wouldn't notice but he probably would, she thought with chagrin. Those calculating green eyes of his never seemed to miss much.

He rejoined her a few moments later in the wheelhouse and he reached up and turned the radio off.

'I was listening to that!' she complained.

'You can listen to it later. Right now I'd rather talk.'

She gave him a quick, warning glance. 'If it's about Jimmy and your sister I don't want to hear it. Talk about anything else but not them.'

'All right. We'll talk about you.' He suddenly moved behind her and her eyes widened in shock as his hands slid round and cupped her breasts.

She clung to the wheel and gulped. 'Stop that! What do you think you're doing?'

'Passing the time in the pleasantest way I can think of in the circumstances.' His voice was low and vibrant behind her ear.

Beneath her thin T-shirt and flimsy bra she could feel herself swelling in response and he grunted with pleasure. 'You have a body that cries out to be caressed and fondled, Carrie. You can't deny what I can feel for myself.'

Her legs trembled and she arced her back as his warm lips brushed the sensitive skin on her neck, sending delicious tremors the length of her spine.

'Don't...' she moaned. 'Please, Nikos...no more...'

Ignoring her mumbled and almost incoherent plea, his lips continued to nibble at her ear and neck. His hands left her breasts and she gasped as they dropped lower and insinuated themselves under her T-shirt. The muscles of her flat stomach tensed and jumped as his fingertips massaged her naked flesh gently.

In harsh desperation she pleaded once more, 'Please, Nikos... Stop it now.'

His fingers were now inserting themselves under the waist of her jeans. 'Do you really want me to stop, Carrie?' he whispered seductively in her ear. 'I'm not hurting you or harming you in any way, am I? I'm giving you something you've denied yourself too long—sensual pleasure.'

He was going to give her a heart attack, she thought despairingly. Her ears were pounding and the blood was sizzling in her veins. Letting go the wheel, she clamped her fingers around his wrists and forced his hands away.

With a sigh of regret, he stopped his provocative behaviour and leaned against the side-window with folded arms and a faint gleam of mockery in the depths of his eyes. 'A pity. I was enjoying that,' he drawled.

'Well, pardon me for spoiling your fun,' she said in a voice that still hadn't quite recovered. 'Keep your hands to yourself in future.'

'I will,' he said drily. 'Until I'm invited, that is. Which you can't keep putting off much longer.'

Grimly she stared ahead, refusing to acknowledge that that possibility even existed.

He changed the subject abruptly. 'Your freight charges are too low. As far as I can work it out you're barely going to cover your running costs on this trip.'

'How I run my business is no concern of yours,' she retorted coldly.

He acknowledged the point with a sardonic smile. 'Agreed. But as a businessman myself I'm intrigued to know how you manage to remain solvent.'

She wished he'd go away and stop bothering her. He was still too damned close. And how did he always manage to look so cool? Her forehead and nose were shiny with perspiration and it was doing nothing for her self-esteem.

His eyes kept questioning her and she knew he'd just keep prodding until he got an answer. She gave a shrug. 'My charges are low because my customers are mostly poor peasants. Just like those two old men up there.' She made a sweeping gesture with her hand. 'There are over two thousand islands out there but most of them are too small and sparsely populated for the regular ferries to bother about.' She brushed a lock of damp hair off her forehead with the back of her hand and went on scathingly, 'No one bothers about those poor devils. It's the tourists with the money they're interested in. Give them cheap plonk and a second-rate bouzouki player in a tatty taverna and they think they've seen Greece. People like you should be ashamed of what's happening out here on the islands. You're neglecting one of the oldest and finest cultures in the world.'

His eyes narrowed. 'People like me?'

'That's right!' She was on her high horse now and ready to give it full rein. 'The landowners . . . the shipowners . . . the people with power.'

His voice cut at her like a whip. 'I'm a Spirakis. My family doesn't need outsiders coming here and lecturing us on our responsibilities.'

The chilling blast of his condemnation robbed her of speech and she felt herself quaking under the force of his anger. The consternation on her face seemed to mollify him and at last his lips stretched in a grim smile of satisfaction. 'Only a fool would believe such a sweeping statement. It might surprise you to know that I agree with everything you say. The smaller communities have been neglected for far too long and there's no doubt that you're performing a valuable social service.'

'Yes . . .' she muttered. 'I'm glad you see it that way.'

His anger lingered a moment longer then he said drily, 'The point I was trying to make is that even a charity has to make enough profit to pay the overheads. There's more to running a boat than recovering the cost of the fuel.' He ticked the items off one by one on his fingers. 'There's depreciation. Maintenance. Harbour dues where necessary. Insurance . . .'

She looked away guiltily and snapped, 'I've already told you that it has nothing to do with you. Just forget it, will you?'

He looked at her thoughtfully. 'If you've managed to survive this long then there's only one answer. You're cutting corners somewhere.'

She bit her lip and fixed her eyes on the horizon ahead.

He continued to stare at her in an unnerving silence then he said quietly, 'Insurance. That's the answer, isn't it?'

'I don't know what you're talking about,' she muttered angrily.

'Don't you?' he taunted. 'That's why you wanted the piano in the hold. You've no cargo insurance. You've never lost a cargo yet and you don't intend to. That's what you told me? The truth is that you can't afford to lose a cargo because it would ruin you.'

Anger compounded by guilt bubbled up inside her and she looked at him resentfully. 'Why should you care whether I'm ruined or not? I thought that was why you came here in the first place.'

'We'll talk about you later,' he promised coldly. 'It's your hypocrisy that surprises me. What about those "poor peasants" you profess to care so much about? If the worst happened and they lost their few pitiful possessions at sea how would you manage to repay them?'

'My unofficial insurance fund would take care of that,' she snapped.

'Unofficial insurance fund? What kind of animal is that?'

She owed him no explanations whatsoever but she was goaded to wipe that smile of cynical disbelief off his face. 'I'm just like you, Mr Spirakis. I don't need a stranger coming here and lecturing me on my responsibilities. I never carry a cargo that is worth more than the amount of money I keep in my bank account. My customers know that. They trust me to make good on any losses. So far it hasn't been necessary and because I don't have to pay inflated premiums to some crooked insurance company I pass the savings on by charging lower freight rates.'

He stood there digesting her explanation in silence and she muttered, 'I don't suppose it's strictly legal. No doubt you can't wait to report it to the authorities.'

'Now what makes you think I'd do a thing like that, Carrie?' he asked with unexpected softness. 'The more I learn about you, the more I realise how similar we are in nature. When it comes to something close to our hearts neither of us minds bending the rules, do we?'

By two o'clock that afternoon they'd reached their destination and unloaded their cargo. An hour later they were heading north-west to pick up another order when the storm descended on them.

The first sign was the sudden drop in temperature that put goose-pimples on Carrie's arms then she saw the ripples disturbing the calm surface of the sea. A moment later Nikos stepped into the wheelhouse and scanned the horizon to the north through the binoculars. 'You were right about the Meltemi,' he muttered. 'Here it comes.'

The wheel gave a sudden kick under her hands as the first gust hit the *Miranda* on the starboard bow. She eased the wheel over and the bows started to rise and fall. It was a gentle motion at first but as the wind gathered strength the waves became higher. Confidently she steered the *Miranda* straight into the wind. Over her shoulder she said, 'There's no telling how long this will last. It would be a good idea to fill the Thermos flasks with hot coffee while we have the chance.'

He grunted in her ear and left the wheelhouse. His easygoing acquiescence surprised and pleased her. She'd half expected him to come the macho bit, grab the wheel and tell her that making coffee was woman's work.

The wind began to flex its muscles. Experience had taught her to judge its strength by the noise it made gusting around the exposed wheelhouse. At the moment it was a low, keening moan—nothing to worry about.

The wind gradually began to increase and the first smatterings of spray lashed against the front window. The *Miranda*, built to withstand a lot worse than this, battered her way blithely through the heaving swell and Carrie felt the familiar thrill of pitting her skill against the elements. This was where the new engine Nikos had installed would prove its worth or not, because if they lost power the *Miranda* would be pushed helplessly broadside to the towering seas and that would be the end.

The keening moan went up a pitch to an angry howl and another, more violent lump of water hurled itself against the wheelhouse.

The sea began breaking over the bows and rushing in torrents along the deck. The *Miranda* began to buck heavily, her bows rising high in the air then crashing down to bury themselves in the following wave. For the first time she felt her mouth go dry. Surely it couldn't get any worse than this.

Nikos returned to the wheelhouse and jammed the two flasks under the chart shelf.

'It's getting pretty rough!' he shouted in her ear. 'Is she handling all right?'

She braced herself as the *Miranda* poised herself for another roller-coaster ride. 'She . . . she's fine. No problem. I told you she was well built.'

'I hope so,' he growled. 'This is going to get a lot worse.' He pressed his face close to the glass to survey the deck then he shouted, 'The tarpaulin over the hold has come loose. I'll have to go out and tie it.'

She looked at the storm-lashed deck then turned to him in horror. 'You're crazy! You can't go out there! You'll be washed overboard.'

'I'll have to!' he yelled back at her. 'If the sea gets into the hold we'll sink.' His face became grave and his eyes held hers. 'I'll have to depend on you, Carrie. I'll be all right if you keep the *Miranda* into the wind. Have you got the strength to do that?'

Her eyes faltered and she ran her tongue nervously over her lips. 'I . . . I think so.'

He gave her a slow, confident grin. 'Of course you can. Even if you can just prevent her rolling until I get that tarpaulin secured. That's all that matters.'

She reached out in a half-hearted effort to stop him but he swung himself out, dropped to the deck and went at a crouching run towards the hold. Watching through the window, she gasped as a torrent of water swept him off his feet. The *Miranda* reared skywards again, shedding its burden of sea, and Nikos was once again visible, flat on his stomach and clinging grimly to the base of the derrick. As the boat reached the crest of the gigantic wave he struggled to his feet and raced towards the combing surrounding the hold.

Fighting against the tight band of panic in her chest, Carrie strained with the wheel. If the *Miranda* turned broadside and rolled Nikos would have no chance. She caught sight of him for a second before the bows buried themselves deep in the next wave and she uttered up a silent prayer.

This was her fault, she realised bitterly. It had been her job to make sure the tarpaulin was securely over the hold after they'd unloaded. Hadn't she been the one who'd predicted this storm? But if she'd known it was going to be as violent as this she'd have stayed in harbour. Even the huge ferries wouldn't put to sea in conditions like this. She recalled her boast to Nikos about the *Miranda* being able to handle anything the Aegean could throw at her. Perhaps the old Greek gods had heard her and were now teaching her a lesson in humility.

The seconds and minutes dragged by to the howling and crashing accompaniment of the elemental fury and she almost choked in relief as Nikos made it safely back to the wheelhouse. Soaked and with his chest heaving, he braced himself against the side-window and met her unspoken query with a nod to indicate that the job was done. After a moment he recovered his breath and tapped her on the shoulder. 'I'll take the wheel for a spell. See if you can pour a mugful of that coffee.'

This time she was glad to hand it over. Her arms felt as if they needed splints and she doubted if she could have held the course much longer. She managed to pour the coffee from the Thermos without spilling too much and she used one hand to steady herself while she held the cup to his lips.

He sipped gratefully and she kept offering it to him until the cup was empty and then she poured one for herself. 'That was . . .' The remark died and the cup fell from her nerveless fingers as she caught sight of the huge wall of water rearing up on them. With a squeal of horror she threw her arms around Nikos's waist and clung to him like a limpet. One thought wiped every other from her mind. This was the end! When that wave crashed down on them it would smash the *Miranda* to matchwood.

There was a tremendous roar and a clap like thunder and she felt the floor of the wheelhouse jolt beneath her feet. Water poured through the shattered roof and as she pressed her cheek against Nikos's back she could feel the muscles and tendons writhing as he fought to control the wheel.

Then somehow, miraculously, the wall of water was astern of them and the *Miranda*, shaken and only slightly wounded, continued plugging ahead. Shamefaced at her display of fear, she unwound her arms and was about to straighten up when he yelled, 'You'd better hang on! We're in more trouble! There's something wrong with the steering.'

Glancing over his shoulder, she could see the *Miranda*'s bows swinging to port while Nikos strained to turn the wheel. In the grip of the wind the boat began to list sideways until the port rail was almost under water then sluggishly she began to answer the helm. This time she went too far to starboard and with a curse Nikos heaved the wheel in the other direction.

'Something's broken!' he shouted. 'Either the rudder is loose or the steering linkage has been damaged.'

White-faced with fear, she stood next to him and grabbed the wheel. 'I'll give you a hand,' she shouted. She wasn't sure how much her puny strength would help but it was better than standing doing nothing.

He looked down at her, a grim smile on his face. 'Thanks.'

The storm lasted another hour. As suddenly as it had begun it blew itself out. The wind went to a low moan then died with a whimper, the waves subsided and the *Miranda* staggered over the calm sea like a punch-drunk boxer.

Carrie almost collapsed with relief against the side of the wheelhouse and she let go a trembling sigh of weariness. 'Thank God that's over.'

His face was finely drawn and lined with fatigue but he managed to give her a smile of encouragement. 'You did well, Carrie.'

She shook her head, a little embarrassed by the uncalled-for praise. 'No, I didn't. I was scared stiff.'

'You think I wasn't? Anyway, we'll have to find some place to tie up so that I can assess the damage. I may be able to repair it myself, depending on how bad it is.' He pointed out of the starboard window. 'That looks like a small island about three miles away. Have a look through the glasses.'

Her hands were still shaking as she peered through the binoculars but finally she was able to tell him with certainty, 'There's no sign of habitation. The shore looks rocky but there's a sandy inlet at the southern end.'

She watched as once more his sinewy arms strained at the wheel as he coaxed the reluctant *Miranda* on to her new course. At that point she should have left him to it and gone out on deck to inspect for further damage but she seemed to be rooted to the spot. Something was happening to her. Something scary. It was as if their brush with disaster had imposed an entirely new dimension on their relationship and as her eyes lingered on him the emotion that swelled in her heart was as sudden and frightening as the storm they'd just escaped.

She averted her eyes and handed him his jeans as he clambered back over the stern rail. No sooner had they dropped anchor in the sheltered inlet than he'd stripped and dived overboard to inspect the rudder. The casual way he'd gone about it hadn't been quite so shocking as the first time. With more insight into his character by now, she thought she was beginning to understand him. Nikos Spirakis was a man who made his own rules and acted as he thought fit regardless of anyone else. His self-assurance was firmly based in a belief in his own strength and rigid set of principles. He just didn't give a damn for negative attitudes like false modesty.

'There's nothing wrong with the rudder,' he informed her. 'It must be the linkage. Do you have a plan of the ship?'

He was tightening his belt when she looked at him again. 'Yes. It's on the shelf above Jimmy's bunk. I'll go and fetch it.'

Once he had the drawing he had no difficulty in determining the probable site of the problem.

'You'll never get in there,' she protested when he removed the cover and showed her the narrow tunnel housing the steering linkage to the rudder. She eyed his wide shoulders. 'You'll get stuck.'

He shrugged. 'The choice is simple. Either I attempt it or we stay here and wait for some passing ship to come to our aid. That might take anything up to a week . . .' He paused and something devilish moved in the depths of his green eyes. 'You don't suppose it was fate that brought us here, do you, Carrie?'

'Fate?' She didn't like the sound of this.

'An ideal spot. Secluded . . . no chance of being disturbed——'

'It's dark in that tunnel,' she said quickly. 'I'll get you a torch.'

Five minutes later, armed with the torch in one hand and a wrench in the other, he wriggled himself head first into the opening. Inch by inch his upper body disappeared, then his legs and finally his feet.

For a moment or two she paced around with a feeling of absolute helplessness. That was going to be the hardest part to bear, the knowledge that there was nothing she could do to make his job easier. She'd derived a lot of satisfaction out of watching him toiling up and down Kati's hill with the water but this was different. The conditions in that tunnel must be hellish. Hot...airless...claustrophobic as a sealed coffin.

Bending down, she called up, 'Nikos? Are you all right?'

The answer was a muffled grunt and she bit her lip. What if something happened to him? What if he got cramp, or passed out through lack of air? How would she get him out? Crawl in, tie a rope around his ankles and drag his inert body out? No. That certainly didn't sound like a feasible proposition.

Dammit! She should have stopped him. She'd put his life in danger because she'd been too scared to spend a week here alone with him. She knew what would happen. Even if he did act as if he had more respect for her now she doubted if that would deflect him from his original plan. It was going to happen sooner or later so why not here? Anyway...could she afford to deny him any longer? She was in danger of forgetting the most important thing of all and that was to have Jimmy returned to her safe and sound.

'Nikos!' she yelled up the tunnel again and was answered by a fainter reply. It sounded as if he was somewhere in the bowels of the earth.

She thought about going to make some coffee because he'd be needing it when he came out and she was on the point of leaving when she hesitated. Suppose something happened and he started shouting for help while she was gone? Indecisively she squatted by the end of the tunnel and nibbled at her thumbnail.

Suddenly she heard a banging noise and then a few moments later Nikos was yelling at her from a million miles away, 'Go to the wheelhouse. See if the wheel is any freer.'

Obediently she ran to the wheelhouse and spun the wheel backwards and forwards then she returned to the end of the tunnel and shouted in, 'It's free.'

'Good. I'm coming out.'

The tension drained from her and with a feeling of deep relief she watched as he slowly emerged feet first. Then his legs were free, then his hips, and then her feeling of relief turned to one of tender pity when she saw the condition he was in. The bruises and lacerations on his back and shoulders were clearly visible beneath the coating of oil and grease.

When he was completely out he straightened up painfully and flexed his cramped joints and muscles. 'One of the rods had buckled,' he explained. 'I managed to fix it.'

'You need a hot shower,' she observed, looking him up and down.

'Yes. I need a hot shower,' he agreed. He glanced down at his chest and stomach, which were every bit as bad as his back. 'I'm not going to argue with that.'

She took a deep breath and tried to keep her voice businesslike. 'You go below now. I'll be down in five minutes.'

The devil was back in his green eyes again. 'Are we going to shower together?'

'No, we're not,' she retorted. 'But your back is in a terrible state. You won't be able to wash it properly by yourself. And I'll need to put some antiseptic cream on those cuts.'

He gave a slow, ironic nod. 'I see. This is your natural maternal instinct crying out, is it? Or does the prospect of touching my body fill you with excitement?'

She flushed at the suggestion and said angrily, 'I'm only trying to be helpful but if that's what you think of me then go ahead and get blood poisoning for all I care.'

He raised a placating hand. 'All right. I apologise. It's just that I find your sudden concern for my welfare a bit surprising. During the storm it was understandable but I can't help wondering what your motive is now. Nevertheless it's appreciated.' A smile of gentle mockery flitted across his face then he said gravely, 'I'll expect you in five minutes.'

As she watched him disappear down the hatchway she unclenched her fists. That was what happened when you felt sorry for someone and tried to help them, she thought bitterly. Perhaps she'd put sand in the ointment just to teach him a lesson.

The accommodation on the *Miranda* was no larger than it had been in her days as a fishing boat with a crew of four but the layout had been altered. The steps down led to the galley, which contained nothing more than a sink, a small Calorgas cooker and a gas-operated fridge. There was a bolted-down table and bench of plain wood. Forward of that were the 'cabins', which were merely two curtained-off sections, each containing a bunk and simple dressing-table and wardrobe. Forward of the cabins another curtained-off section contained the toilet and shower.

As she approached it now she could hear the hiss of water and see the clouds of steam rising. Standing next to the curtain, she shouted his name. 'Nikos!'

The plastic curtain was pulled aside and he blinked the water from his eyes. 'You're early.'

Knowing him by now, she'd been prepared for this, and she looked at him calmly. 'No, I'm not. Now please turn round and face the wall.'

When he'd reluctantly complied with her order she worked up a lather on her hands with the soap and then ran them gently over his shoulders and up and down his back.

'I'm not hurting you, am I?' she asked.

He turned his head sideways and growled, 'I didn't even know you'd started. Rub harder, woman. I'm not a delicate ornament.'

Narrowing her eyes, she reached up and dug her fingers into the hard flesh of his shoulders and kneaded it vigorously.

'Is that better?'

'Perfect. Do that all over and I'll feel like a new man.'

Five minutes later she stopped and said, 'That's as far as I'm going. You can do the rest yourself. When you've made yourself respectable come down to the galley and I'll put the ointment on your back.'

Her own clothes were still damp from the storm, and the splashing from the shower hadn't helped. In the privacy of her 'cabin' she stripped off and changed, then she went to the galley and filled the chipped enamel coffee-pot.

The thought that had occurred to her earlier now returned to torment her. Perhaps Nikos was right and it really was fate that had driven the *Miranda* to this secluded inlet. As he'd said, it was an ideal spot. And she'd only been delaying the inevitable. And let's face up to it, Carrie, she thought; I mean, let's at least be honest and admit it. You're burning up for him, aren't you? If he took you in his arms right now you'd surrender without a murmur of protest. Yes, but . . .

Yes, but. That was the trouble, wasn't it? she thought bleakly. He was ready enough to tease and raise her to fever pitch but the ultimate decision was to be hers and hers alone. That was the price of Jimmy's freedom. She was the one who'd have to do the asking!

She knew only too well what would happen then. He'd accept the spoils of his victory but in his heart he'd despise her. After all, that was his stated intention, wasn't it? To punish her brother by humiliating her. But if she allowed that to happen she'd earn nothing but his scorn and contempt, and that would be too hard to bear because she was beginning to care what he thought about her! For some utterly insane reason she was falling in love with the impossible creature.

She'd just finished brewing the coffee when she heard his soft footfalls approaching the galley and with a deep breath she pulled herself together. He was wearing nothing but a pair of clean jeans. Gesturing at the bench, she said, 'Sit astride that.'

She poured him a hot, sweet coffee then settled herself on the bench behind him and dipped her fingers into the ointment. 'This may sting a bit,' she said apologetically.

He sipped his coffee unconcernedly and gently she applied the cream to the worst of the abrasions and cuts. 'Are...are you sure I'm not hurting you?' she asked.

'Only my patience,' he growled. 'Get on with it.'

Biting her lip, she went on with the treatment.

'There,' she said firmly. 'That should stop any infection.'

He flexed his stiff shoulders then turned on the bench to sit facing her. 'What about the scratches on my chest and stomach?'

Her gaze dropped away. 'You can do those yourself.'

He held up his hands which were clasping the mug of coffee. 'I can't. As you can see, my hands are full.'

Hiding her discomfort behind a sarcastic smile, she dipped her fingers into the ointment once more and said, 'Well, we can't keep the lord and master from his well earned coffee, can we?'

She dealt with his chest first, her fingers gliding over the smooth skin and her mind desperately trying to distance itself from the feeling of dark excitement coursing through her body.

Lower down there was a long scratch across the taut flatness of his stomach and by now her blood-pressure was putting a pink flush on her face.

When that had been seen to he unbuckled his belt and loosened the waist of his jeans. 'What about this one?'

She gulped as she saw the other scratch running downwards from his navel and as she tenderly applied the ointment she felt that strange aching weakness in her thighs. Quickly she got to her feet and said with forced brightness, 'Well, that's you taken care of. Now I think you should——' She gave a gasp of surprise as he grabbed her wrist and pulled her down to the bench again.

'Don't be in such a hurry.' His voice was pleasant but insistent. 'All good nurses should take time off to chat with their patients. It's good for morale, they say.'

The smile she gave back was also pleasant—and wary. 'I'm not a nurse. I only put some——'

'But you have the heart and the hands of a nurse,' he went on in a voice pitched deliberately low and vibrant. 'Tender and caring.' He released her suddenly then eyed her with blatant provocation. 'Those hands of yours were the first thing I noticed when we first met. Your hands and your cornflower-blue eyes. There wasn't much else of you visible, I grant. Only an oil-streaked face that might or might not have been beautiful.'

'Yes, well, let's forget that, shall we?' She looked away in embarrassment and quickly changed the subject. 'There's nothing more I can do here. I'm going up to repair the roof on the wheelhouse.'

His eyes continued to dwell on her, in disturbing, contemplative silence, then he got to his feet. 'That's a man's job. I'll do it. You can look in the fridge and decide what we're going to have for dinner this evening.'

As soon as he'd gone she released a long, trembling breath and wiped the perspiration from her brow. It would have to be tonight. She couldn't hold out any longer. She looked at the pot of coffee and shook her head. What she needed was two large double brandies. Instead she settled for a long hot shower.

CHAPTER FIVE

CARRIE had put it off as long as she could and when she went up on deck some time later the sun was getting ready to dip below the western horizon. The last rays were turning the sands of the inlet a deep rosy pink and the first star of the evening was shining in the east. She took a deep breath of the fragrant air then spread the blankets on the deck by the side of the wheelhouse. When she looked up she saw Nikos grinning down at her.

'They're to sit on,' she explained calmly. 'I thought we'd have our meal on deck. It's too warm below.'

For a moment she could almost feel his eyes surgically peeling away at her skin layer by layer until he could read her very soul, then he murmured lazily, 'That sounds like a very good idea, Carrie. I can tell that this is going to be a meal to remember.'

Still struggling to maintain a pretence of normality, she said, 'It'll be dark in a few minutes. There are a couple of storm lanterns in the wheelhouse locker.'

His lips stretched in a smile of anticipation. 'I'll fetch them. I like to see what I'm . . . eating.'

When she went below again she made straight for her cabin and studied her reflection nervously in the mirror. Hurriedly she applied the brush again to her long blonde hair and retied it with a fresh black ribbon. Still not satisfied with her appearance but realising that it was too late now to do anything about it, she returned to the galley. Checking that everything they'd need for the meal was in the basket, she took a deep breath then carried it up to the deck.

Nikos had hung the two storm lanterns on the side of the wheelhouse. He'd also switched on the radio and the strains of the Vienna Philharmonic, courtesy of an Athens radio station, floated gently on the evening air. Laying down the basket, she walked to the stern and drank in the view.

The spectacular sunset had also drawn Nikos and they stood side by side in reverent silence watching the fiery descent into the sea. Darkness followed swiftly as the sky turned from crimson to deep purple. One by one the stars came out and the sea slumbered peacefully, tired, no doubt, after its exhausting day.

Neither of them spoke as they made their way back along the deck. In the soft yellow light of the lanterns she squatted on the blanket and opened the basket. Pulling out the wine and the glasses, she handed him the bottle. 'You pour.'

He held it up to the light and read the label. 'Danielis! Well, you're full of little surprises, aren't you?'

'I have a crate of the stuff,' she told him casually. 'It was part-payment for a job I did. I only bring it out on special occasions.'

He raised an innocent eyebrow. 'And what special occasion are we celebrating tonight?'

She gave a delicate shrug of her shoulders. 'Our deliverance from the storm? I'd call that a reason for celebrating, wouldn't you?' Without waiting for an answer, she brought out a large dish and lifted the cover. 'Cold chicken and orange segments. That's the best I could do.'

When he nodded in approval she forked a large helping on to a plate and handed it to him. 'There's plenty of tinned stuff but none of it goes with the wine.' It was a pretty feeble joke made in an attempt to hide her nervousness but she had a feeling that it was a waste of time. Anyway, she was entitled to feel nervous, wasn't she? Just exactly how did you go about asking a man to make love to you?

Perhaps the wine would help, she thought as she watched him pour. A couple of bottles of that stuff should be enough to make her lose her inhibitions. As far as she could recall remaining sober hadn't been part of the deal.

He looked even more devastating than usual sitting there, she thought. Something to do with the lantern glow...and the starlight...and the deep shadows on his chest...and the... She tore her eyes away before he made some comment about the way she was staring at him.

'We can make an early start in the morning,' she said, trying to get a casual conversation going. 'Make up for lost time.'

'We might,' he drawled lazily. 'Then again we might grow to like this place, and if I can find some way of amusing myself...well...who knows?'

'A-amuse yourself?'

He just smiled at her enigmatically and speared another piece of chicken.

This was ridiculous, she thought. He knew damn well what was going to happen and he was deliberately making it as difficult as possible for her. Surely he wasn't going to stick to the letter of his threat? He wasn't going to wait until she got down on her knees and pleaded with him, was he? Good God! Maybe he was.

His green eyes seemed to be glowing at her in the dark. Just like a tiger's. A jungle predator ready to pounce and devour its victim.

Steeling herself, she put her hand out. 'Nikos?'

She prayed for him to take it and pull her roughly towards him. Her heart was hammering and her body aching.

He looked at her hand for a moment then straight into her eyes. 'Yes, Carrie?'

'Do...do you want...want to——?' Her voice broke. The words just wouldn't come. They'd never come—not without help.

'Want to what, Carrie?' he asked softly.

He was enjoying this cat-and-mouse game, she thought bleakly. It suited a man of his type to watch his victims squirm.

The tortured silence stretched between them until he said with mock-sympathy, 'You seem to have lost your tongue. You want some more wine, is that it?' He took her glass and refilled it. 'It's nothing to feel embarrassed about. It's a very good wine. I'm going to have some more myself.'

Her hand shook as she took the glass from him, then she turned her head away from those searching eyes. What kind of dark and potent power did this man have? He was a callous, cold-hearted devil, so why, in spite of everything, did she still feel this maddening desire to be in his arms and feel his lips on hers? There was no use pretending that this had anything to do with saving Jimmy. This was for her and her alone. So why? Was it some flaw in her character—some in-built self-destruct button?

Nikos finished his meal then pushed his plate to the side and helped himself to another glass. 'The hourly news bulletin was on the radio while you were below,' he remarked casually. 'They were describing the storm. It seems to have been even worse than we thought.'

Something in his tone made her forget her own problems for a moment. There was an affinity between people like her who made their living on the sea and the fate of one touched them all. 'Were there any casualties?' she asked quickly.

He shook his head. 'Fortunately no. But there was a lot of damage. The Skipos ferry ran aground and at least a dozen yachts capsized.' He paused then looked at her significantly. 'I could have been a casualty. It's only thanks to you that I wasn't.'

'Thanks to me?' Her blue eyes questioned him. As far as she was concerned it had been the other way around. If it hadn't been for the risks he'd taken and his superhuman efforts with the damaged steering neither of them would be here.

'When I went out on deck to tie the tarpaulin over the hold you fought like a devil to keep the *Miranda* on an even keel. If you'd allowed the boat to roll I'd undoubtedly have been swept over the side.' His brows were drawn together and his eyes were demanding an answer. 'That was your chance to get rid of me, Carrie. Why didn't you take it?

No one would ever have known that it was anything other than an accident.'

The question rocked her and she stared at him in incredulity. 'Are you actually asking me why I didn't . . . didn't kill you?'

He shrugged. 'Why not? I've given you no cause to like me. Quite the opposite, in fact.'

My God, she thought! He was serious! What kind of person did he think she was? She found her voice at last. 'Well,' she said, stiff with indignation, 'if you think I'm capable of a thing like that you're an abysmal judge of character. Perhaps the Spirakis family live by the law of the jungle but where I come from people have risen above that kind of thing.'

His studied her with that familiar dark frown then he sighed. 'I can see that you're genuinely offended. Please accept my apologies. When one is constantly surrounded by enemies one almost constantly expects the worst.'

'I'm not surprised you're surrounded by enemies,' she muttered. 'You don't exactly go out of your way to be pleasant, do you?'

His eyes glinted dangerously. 'I'm trying to be pleasant at the moment, Carrie. Don't make it too hard for me.'

Oh, God forbid, she thought drily. Don't make things too hard for him? That had to be the joke of the month, surely. 'All right.' She sighed. 'I accept your apology. Now let's talk no more about it.'

He leaned a little closer. 'Thank you, Carrie. But the fact remains that you saved my life and I can't dismiss a thing like that lightly. I feel honour-bound to reward you in some way.'

She eyed him warily. 'Reward? I don't want any reward from you unless it's a promise to let my brother go.'

He moved even closer. 'We'll talk about that later. For the time being perhaps you'd be good enough to accept a kiss as a token of my gratitude?'

'A kiss?' Her mouth was suddenly dry. 'You . . . you want to kiss me?'

'Just as a token of my gratitude,' he repeated softly.

His face was very close to hers now. So close that she felt herself being drawn into and sucked under by those deep green eyes. 'Go . . . go on, then,' she stammered. 'If that's what you really want.'

His hand came up and gently touched the smooth skin of her cheek. 'I think it's what we both want, Carrie,' he whispered.

He was so close now that their thighs were touching, then, still caressing her cheek with one hand, he placed his lips lightly on hers. For a moment his mouth remained still, the pressure hardly felt, then his other hand came up to cup her other cheek. Holding her head perfectly still between his hands, he moved his lips lightly over hers, side to side, in a slow, sensual rhythm that both teased and tormented. She began to tremble and instinctively she gripped his shoulders for support.

Now he increased the pressure and her heart began a demented pounding in her ears. Deep within the dim recesses of her soul the familiar dark demon was coming awake and stirring her blood, heating it and sending it rushing through her system. Her lips parted at the first touch of his tongue and she lost herself in the sweet sensation as it entered and explored its willing receptacle.

Her heart gave an extra thud as his arms went around her and pulled her down. Then he was half on top of her, his weight pinning her helplessly to the blanket. His tongue ceased wreaking its havoc in her mouth and he looked into the depths of her eyes. 'I want to make love to you, Carrie.'

She tried to speak. She tried again then gave up and managed a weak nod.

'If you resist I'll stop.' His lips brushed against her eyelids and his breath was warm and sweet on her cheek. 'I promised not to take you by force and I won't.'

She didn't even attempt to speak this time. In desperation her hands entwined themselves behind his neck and she pulled his mouth once more towards hers in a wanton greed that was utterly new and almost frightening in its intensity. It was a greed, however, that demanded more than his mouth, and her fingers raked down his back in a blind craving that was suddenly arrested by his stifled gasp of pain.

Oh, God! The abrasions on his back! She'd forgotten all about them in her blinding desire. 'Nikos...I'm sorry. I didn't mean to hurt you,' she whispered in a voice of tortured guilt.

He eased himself off her and her heart plummeted. He didn't believe her! He thought she'd done it deliberately.

'Please, Nikos,' she begged. 'It was an accident. I didn't mean... It was an accident. I forgot...'

Her voice trailed off as he suddenly kneeled astride her and pressed his finger to her lips.

'I know you didn't mean to,' he assured her gently. 'Let's just say that you were carried away by your passion. Your punishment is to lie perfectly still for the next five minutes. Are you capable of doing it, my little tigress with claws?'

She gazed up into his fathomless eyes, searching the hidden depths for some hint of his intentions, then she nodded in dumb acquiescence.

'Good.' He laid his hands on her waist and slid them under her T-shirt. 'So much beauty shouldn't be hidden from view, Carrie.' She could feel him raising her T-shirt and gently easing it over her upthrust breasts. At his soft command she obediently raised her arms and a moment later the garment was off and cast aside. With no prompting she arced her back and allowed him to unfasten her bra and when that also was cast aside she lay naked from the waist up, shamelessly basking in his gaze of wonder and admiration. A feeble voice from her conscience condemned her outrageous conduct but stronger emotions shouted it down and told it to mind its own business.

Almost reverentially he laid a hand on each of her breasts, feeling the firmness and the already gorged nipples, dark brown against her creamy skin. 'Aphrodite!' he murmured. 'Truly the body of a goddess.'

Moving backwards, he slowly unzipped her jeans and slid them down over her hips and her long, tapering legs. Wearing nothing now but her wispy briefs, she closed her eyes and trembled with a delicious anticipation as that final article was removed. She opened them in time to watch as he undressed himself then her arms reached upwards to pull him down beside her. As their mouths met again in moist collision she felt the hardness of his body against her own yielding flesh and the contact sent shivers of desire through her limbs.

Finally his mouth, like some beloved vandal, left hers and traced a path down to her throat to goad the wildly fluttering pulse, then it continued down, leaving a trail of scorched and battered nerve-endings, until it found its ultimate destination, pounced and voraciously plundered her nipple. Her fingers convulsively curled themselves in his dark hair and a groan of sensual pleasure escaped her swollen lips.

Her flesh quivered as his right hand began a tender exploration over the contours of her stomach and hips then she moaned again as it gently parted her thighs and slid upwards to claim its prize.

She could hear the breath rasping harsh and urgent in his throat as he rolled on top of her. His left hand slid under her buttocks to raise her up and she curled her lower lip between her teeth to stifle the cry as he thrust himself into her. For a moment he lay still and she felt crushed by his weight until he raised himself and used his fore-arms as support. Afraid to hurt his back again, she held him firmly by the hair as if afraid that he'd get up and leave her lying there, a gasping, shuddering wreck of cheated passion.

He stared down at her, his green eyes alight with the fire of some inner storm, then he began moving. The slow and rhythmic thrusting evoked a primitive

response in her own body and it aided and abetted this welcome invasion with a rhythm of its own.

Waves of voluptuous pleasure rippled through her body, driving everything before them. Neither time nor space existed. Nothing but this feeling mattered. His thrusts became quicker, as did her responses, raising her to a fevered pitch of frenzy that nothing had ever prepared her for. Then at the last possible moment she heard him groan and felt him shudder and her loins convulsed in a silent explosion of sheer ecstasy and fulfilment.

She clung to his hair until the paroxysm slowly subsided then her arms fell uselessly by her sides and she let out one final long sigh of spent passion.

He kissed her eyelids then her mouth and whispered, 'Did I please you?'

She raised her hand and ran her fingers over his lips. 'What kind of stupid question is that?' she breathed. 'Couldn't you tell?'

He nibbled at her fingertips then murmured, 'The next time will be better. I won't be so impatient.'

She looked up into those glowing green eyes and for the sake of decency assumed a slightly scandalised frown. 'The next time? What makes you think there will be a next time?'

He laughed softly. 'Why should I think there won't?' He rolled on to his side, propped himself up on one elbow and surveyed the length of her body like a man admiring a newly acquired possession. 'I've decided that we'll stay here tomorrow. We'll go ashore and explore the island then later we'll light a fire on the beach and have sex again.'

Have sex? That sounded far too cold and businesslike for her. Why hadn't he said 'make love'? This time her frown was genuine but her doubts were swept aside as he leaned down and kissed her once more.

At some time during the evening he went below and returned with more wine, an extra blanket and two pillows. She was lying just as he'd left her and she pointed a finger towards the stars and suppressed a giggle. 'There are satellites up there. They use infra-red to see in the dark and here are the pair of us as naked as the day we were born. For all we know we might be on a big TV screen in Houston or Moscow.'

He chuckled at the idea. 'As long as it stops them launching rockets at one another.'

Impishly she waved her hand at the sky. 'It gives a whole new meaning to the slogan about making love not war, doesn't it?'

He sat down and poured the wine.

They talked a lot—at least she did. The wine was probably responsible for that and she didn't need much prompting to tell him about her life in England before she'd decided to live permanently in Greece. He seemed especially interested in her father and the way he'd just thrown away a life of dull security to follow a dream.

'He did the right thing,' Nikos asserted gravely. 'A man has only one life. He shouldn't waste it.'

She nodded vigorously. 'That's just what Dad used to say. Never be afraid of tomorrow because tomorrow will be yesterday the day after... I mean... today is the tomorrow you were worried about yesterday. Something like that.'

'I know what he meant,' Nikos said drily. He took the glass from her hand. 'I think you've had enough wine.'

A pleasant drowsiness was stealing over her and she looked at him through heavy, half-closed lids. 'I think you're right. But I'm not drunk. Just a little... tired. You don't mind if I have a little nap, do you?'

'I think we both need some sleep,' he yawned.

'Yes.' She lay down with her head on the pillow and reached up for him lazily. 'Nikos? Do you want to know something really crazy?'

He lay down beside her. 'What might that be?'

'I like you,' she murmured. 'I shouldn't but I can't help it.'

'Hmm. I was right—you have had too much to drink. Now turn over and go to sleep.'

She awoke once during the night. His arm lay lightly across her breast and his breathing was deep and even. For a while she was content to lie on her back gazing at the stars and listening to the gentle lapping of the waves, then her hand touched Nikos's bare thigh. He sighed in his sleep and for a moment she felt an overpowering urge to move her hand and arouse him so that once more she could experience that special kind of heaven only he could provide. Her hand crept across his hip then she hesitated. Perhaps it would be better just to let him sleep on, she thought dreamily. He might not be able to. Not so soon after. She wished she knew more about men. Anyway, there was no point in taking a chance. It might just make him angry. She could wait until tomorrow. She smiled in the darkness. Good God, she was turning into a right little wench, wasn't she? Well, so what? Apart from the brief episode with that rat Victor she'd lived a pretty blameless life up till now. She was entitled to break out now and again. After all, she was only human like everyone else, she told herself.

The sun was up when she next awoke. She sat up and immediately clutched her head in both hands. 'Ohhhh....'

'Feeling rough?'

She squinted through her eyes and saw the tall silhouette by the rail. 'A little,' she muttered. 'It must be what they call a hangover.'

'I know a good cure for that.'

'Coffee and a couple of aspirins will do fine. I'll be right as rain in half an hour.'

Suddenly his shadow fell across her and he scooped her up into her arms. 'This cure is guaranteed instantaneous.'

The intimate contact and warmth of his body brought a surprised smile to her face. 'Nikos! What are you——?' Her question turned into a squeal as he took two swift steps across the deck, then leapt over the rail into the sea.

The initial shock took her breath away and she struggled to the surface spluttering and gasping. 'You...you great baboon. What do you think you're——?' Her indignant outburst was cut short as he wrapped his arms around her and clamped his mouth over hers.

Stuck together like two limpets, they sank below the surface feet first, then when her chest was ready to burst he released her and she shot up to gulp in great lungfuls of air. A moment later he bobbed up beside her, his dark hair plastered over his forehead and his eyes full of wicked mischief.

'How's the headache now?'

Her breath was getting back to normal and although the water was comfortably warm she looked at him resentfully. 'I'd rather have had the coffee and aspirin.'

Still treading water, he pulled her close to his body and grinned. 'This cure is more fun.'

Their lips met again and she felt his hands reach down to clasp her buttocks. She could also feel something else and her eyes widened. 'Nikos! We can't! Not here. We'll drown!'

She felt herself being lifted and he gave another grin. 'No, we won't. Just keep moving your arms.'

Gasping, she wrapped her legs around him and began beating furiously at the water.

Afterwards they swam to the beach and she lay exhausted on the sand. When her nerves had at last settled down she turned on her side and poked him in the ribs. 'You're incredible. I suppose that was your idea of hydrotherapy.'

'Well, I told you it was better than aspirin,' he murmured lazily. 'You didn't drown after all and I'll bet your headache is gone.'

He was lying on his back with his hands clasped behind his head and his eyes closed. She poked him in the ribs again. 'You must have done that before.'

His lips twitched in an enigmatic smile and she felt an irrational twinge of jealousy. How many women had he made love to? she wondered. Fifty? A hundred? Or had he lost count entirely? And how did he rate her on a scale of one to ten? Minus two? He was probably used to more experienced women.

The really hot-blooded, sultry Latin type with dark flashing eyes and seductive smiles.

His voice broke into her thoughts. 'I always thought of Englishwomen as being cold and unemotional until I met you, Carrie. You've made me change my opinion.'

She stared at him in embarrassed silence. He'd been reading her mind! Well, that shouldn't surprise her. One look at those eyes of his and you could tell he was related to the prince of darkness. At least he'd answered her question—yet she wasn't quite sure whether she should treat it as a compliment or not. What was he really trying to say? Had she been too...easy for his liking? Was he disappointed at her lack of resistance? Perhaps he was the kind of man who despised meek surrender because it robbed him of the feeling of 'conquest'. Never mind that he'd blackmailed her into it in the first place. That probably hadn't even occurred to him.

Unwilling to delve any deeper into the quagmire of motivation and analysis, she got to her feet hastily. 'I'm hungry. I'll fix some breakfast and give you a call when it's ready.' She waded out into the water and began swimming towards the *Miranda*.

After breakfast they loaded the dinghy then returned to the beach and began a slow exploration of the island. Climbing to the highest point, they could see nothing but acres of stunted scrub and wild herbs. The soil was thin and poor and Nikos ran it through his fingers then remarked drily that he wasn't surprised that the place was deserted. It was fit for nothing but goats.

'I like it,' she said obstinately. 'I think it's quite beautiful, in fact. It's just the way God made it and no one has come here to despoil it.'

'You regard well tended orchards, fields and olive groves as despoilation, do you?'

She looked into his mocking eyes and retorted defiantly, 'I find them boring.'

'I doubt if the starving millions of this world would share your sentiment.' He laughed at her obvious discomfort. 'That's the difference between you and me, Carrie. You're an idealist, I'm a realist. I know what has to be done and I do it.'

She clamped her mouth shut and kept it firmly shut until they arrived back at the beach. He immediately began searching for wood and when he'd found a suitable length he began sharpening the point. For a while she just sat watching him then her curiosity got the better of her. 'What's that for?'

He tried the point with his finger. 'We haven't got anything decent to eat. I, being the realist, am going to spear some fish for supper while you, my dear little idealist, are busy collecting driftwood for the fire.'

He took her again that night by the glowing embers of the fire. It was sweet. It was tender. It was everything she'd ever dreamed of and more. Just before she fell asleep exhausted in his protective arms she knew that for good or bad she was hopelessly and helplessly in love.

CHAPTER SIX

IT WAS five o'clock on the following evening when they tied the *Miranda* up to the jetty in Thikos harbour, and that was when Carrie found out just how big a fool she'd been and just how much she really meant to Nikos.

She'd first begun to suspect it early that morning when she'd taken coffee up to the wheelhouse. The anchor had been raised and the *Miranda* was just slipping out of the inlet. She had taken one last look at the beach and sighed. 'I won't forget this place in a hurry, Nikos. I'll always remember it as somewhere special.'

He took the coffee from her and gave an uninterested grunt. 'I don't see why. As I told you yesterday, it's fit for nothing but goats.'

Her blue eyes clouded. It was hardly the response she'd expected. More like a slap in the face, really.

'Perhaps you'd be good enough to tell me what course I'm supposed to be steering,' he growled.

She ignored the tone and the hint of irritated sarcasm in his voice and found the chart. 'There,' she said, pointing. 'Thikos. We need fuel, fresh water and provisions and my credit is good there. We'll spend the night there then head north towards——'

'I know Thikos,' he said, cutting her off abruptly. 'There's a good hotel. At least we'll have a comfortable bed for the night.'

'What's the matter?' she asked stiffly. 'Getting tired of roughing it?'

'I just don't see any point in spurning the benefits of civilisation whenever they're available,' he said shortly.

She felt like telling him that she'd never invited him aboard in the first place then thought better of it. It was going to lead to things she was desperately trying not to think about. She bit her lip then said awkwardly, 'Yes...well, I'm going below now to tidy up. I'll take the wheel over in a couple of hours.'

She took her frustration out on the galley floor with a stiff scrubber. All right, she hadn't expected hugs and kisses, but he could have been a bit more polite, a bit less surly. Granted he was right and the place was only fit for goats, but surely it meant more to him than that. It was the place they'd first made love and you'd have thought that at least...

Her knuckles grew white around the handle of the scrubber as the memory suddenly flashed through her mind with sickening clarity. They hadn't made 'love'. Love had nothing to do with it. They'd simply had sex. Those had been his own words. After all, he was a realist and damned proud of it. A spade was a spade and she was being nothing but a damned fool if she tried to read any more into it than that.

She finished the floor then tackled the cooker and by the time she'd finished that she found herself wondering if she was over-reacting. Just because he'd been a bit offhand with her she was jumping to the worst possible conclusions. After all they'd been through together...surely he wasn't still... Too afraid to put the thought into words, she glared around the galley for something else to attack.

Praying that his mood had changed, she took another coffee up to him when she went to relieve him at the wheel. Smiling brightly, she handed him the mug. 'That's the last of the sugar in there, Nikos. I saved it for you.'

He took it with scarcely a murmur and she gently ran the tips of her fingers over his back. 'Those cuts are almost healed. It must have been the...salt water yesterday morning.'

You'd have thought that the oblique reference to their session of 'hydrotherapy' would have caused at least a flicker of amusement, but it didn't. He turned to her briefly but it was long enough for her to see the blank indifference in his eyes as he grunted, 'Yes. I dare say it was.'

Once again she stiffened at his surly rejection of her attempts to be friendly and she said coldly, 'I'll take the wheel now.'

With a shrug he stepped aside and took his coffee out on deck.

Grabbing the wheel and automatically checking the course, she swallowed her bitterness. He'd accused her of being an idealist and maybe she was but when circumstances warranted it she could be just as much a realist as he claimed to be. She could be just as bloody-minded as him. Before this day was over he was going to find that out. She'd given him what he wanted and now it was up to him to stick to his side of the bargain.

As soon as they arrived at Thikos he went ashore to book a room at the hotel, leaving her to see to the refuelling. As for the provisions, she'd see to them first thing in the morning when the produce in the local market was fresh. Finally she topped up the fresh-water tank from the pump on the jetty then she went below for a quick shower.

Ten minutes later she was back on deck again, dressed in a red blouse and white skirt. There was still no sign of him and she paced around the deck impatiently.

Her plan of action was still hazy in her mind but she was determined about one thing. She wasn't going to sleep with him tonight. This farce had gone on long enough. She was through being used by men. Victor had used her for his own gratification and Nikos was simply using her as a way of restoring his 'family honour', whatever that was supposed to mean. Well, it was ending right here and now. The next man who came into her life was going to have a hard time proving that he truly loved her before she'd allow him to lay a finger on her.

When Nikos eventually arrived back she had to spend a quarter of an hour kicking her heels until he'd showered and changed and then, when he came up on deck, he had the nerve to comment on her appearance.

Eyeing her up and down critically, he grunted, 'I like the blouse. The skirt is too short. Haven't you anything a bit less revealing?'

Her hackles rose then she contented herself with a look of scorn. 'You weren't so damned prudish yesterday.'

'Yesterday we were on a deserted island,' he reminded her coldly. 'This is a busy port. I'm well known here.'

She had a ready answer to that. 'Well, if you're afraid it'll hurt your reputation to be seen consorting with a piece of trash like me you can always go by yourself. I'd much rather stay here anyway.'

With a gleam of dark humour in his eyes he gripped her firmly by the arm and yanked her on to the jetty.

The restaurant he took her to was busy but the head waiter, obviously recognising him, conjured up a fairly secluded table and took their order.

In contrast to his attitude towards her during the day, Nikos was all affable charm now. She kept her responses polite but distant during the meal and this time she was careful to stick to her normal limit of two glasses of wine. When he attempted to pour her a third glass she put her hand firmly over the top. 'No, thanks. I've had enough.'

'It's a very good wine,' he pointed out. 'It would be a pity to waste it now that the bottle is open.'

'You drink it. I'm sure you can manage.'

The candlelight reflected in his green eyes as he frowned. 'What's wrong? Aren't you feeling well?'

'Perfectly well, thank you.'

He leaned over the table and lowered his voice, 'Then why are you being so unsociable?'

Her eyes smouldered at him angrily for a moment. 'You haven't been particularly talkative yourself today, have you?'

'I had something on my mind,' he explained sharply. 'Your small talk was distracting me.'

'Well, I've got something on my mind,' she snapped back. 'And your small talk is boring me. I've more important things to think about.'

'I see.' He tapped his knife on his plate and stared at her thoughtfully. 'Perhaps you'd like to tell me about it.'

'Oh, I will,' she promised heavily. 'But not here. I hate creating scenes in restaurants. Somewhere quieter would be more advisable.'

His lips stretched in a thin, humourless smile. 'Such as our hotel room?'

'That'll do perfectly as long as the walls are thick enough.'

'Hmm. It sounds as if I'm going to have a very interesting night.'

Her blue eyes were icy. 'You can bet on it, Mr Spirakis.' Oh, yes, it would be interesting enough, she told herself. But not quite in the way he was expecting.

They finished their meal in silence then Nikos ordered a taxi to take them the short distance to their hotel. As soon as they were in the room he examined the large double bed then smiled at her provocatively. 'I think we'll be quite comfortable on this, Carrie. Shall we get undressed and try it out now?'

'You can do whatever you like,' she told him disdainfully. 'I've no intention of sleeping with you tonight. Or any other night, come to that.'

'Is that a fact?' He considered her statement briefly then fixed her with a penetrating look. 'You realise the consequences to your brother if you take that course of action?'

'I'm through being blackmailed by you,' she grated. 'I gave you what you wanted so now I want you to turn Jimmy free. There's a phone on that table. You can give the order right now.'

'Out of the question,' he said dismissively. 'Now, is there anything else on your mind?'

Her mouth dropped open. She'd been prepared for anything but this granite-hard refusal. He'd spoken and that was that. One look at that coldly set face, the utter lack of sympathy in his eyes was enough to tell her that her act of rebellion was doomed to failure.

White-faced and shaking with impotent anger, she lowered herself into a chair and muttered, 'I've been a fool. I should have known.' She looked up at him with a hopeless bitterness. 'I was falling in love with you. And I thought...' The words stuck in her throat for a moment then she continued, 'I thought you were starting to have...to have feelings for me. But I was wrong, wasn't I? You don't have any feelings at all, do you? You're just like a soulless robot programmed for revenge.'

'You had no business falling in love with me,' he growled. 'You're only complicating matters.'

She was complicating matters? Good God, it was enough to make you break out in hysterical laughter, she thought. Perhaps she should apologise to him for falling in love.

'I've been honest with you right from the start,' he went on ruthlessly. 'The least you can do is be equally honest with yourself.'

'And what the hell is that supposed to mean?' she demanded in a fury.

He strode across the room, gripped her shoulders and pulled her savagely to her feet. 'I'll tell you what it means,' he mouthed. 'You're suffering from a guilty conscience and you're trying to lay the blame on me.'

She looked at him as if he'd gone mad. 'Me? I've done nothing to feel guilty about. You're the one who should be feeling ashamed of yourself.'

'Stop deluding yourself, you little fool,' he rasped. 'Your conscience wants you to play the suffering martyr in order to save your brother but your natural instincts are betraying you. You've found to your horror that you actually want to have sex with me. That's the truth of the matter, isn't it?'

She tried to struggle free from his grip. 'Let me go. You're out of your mind.'

'Answer me!' he demanded fiercely. 'Admit it.'

She glared up at him in frustration then shook her head. 'No. That's ridiculous.'

'Is it?' His green eyes seemed to burn their way into her soul. 'Are you foolish enough to think that a man can't tell when a woman desires him? The look that lingers a fraction too long. The dilated pupils. The slight flush. The way she trembles at your touch. If you'd worn a sign round your neck saying "Take me, I'm yours" you couldn't have made it more obvious.'

She looked away, unable to stand that searching scrutiny any longer. 'Your imagination was playing you tricks,' she muttered angrily. 'Wishful thinking. I never asked you to make love to me. You just grabbed me and I . . . I——'

'You're the one whose imagination and memory is playing tricks,' he broke in coldly. 'I didn't grab you. The fact is that I was feeling sorry for you. My original intention was to make you kneel and plead with me to take you but that was too much to ask. You arrived on deck that night with blankets and pillows and after a few glasses of wine you tried to summon up enough courage. But you couldn't, could you? That's when I decided to make things easier for you by initiating the proceedings. I thanked you for saving my life and asked if I could kiss you.' He paused then went on drily, 'That was all you were waiting for, wasn't it?'

A feeling of self-revulsion swept through her, leaving her sick with humiliation. Had she really been that obvious? That transparent? God, how he must have been laughing to himself.

He released her and she sank down into the chair again. It was hard to decide whom she hated most, him or herself. She saw him go to the phone and for a moment her heart leapt. Perhaps he was going to relent and let Jimmy go at last. Then she heard him tell Room Service to send up two bottles of wine and glasses.

Her blue eyes glittered at him in anger. 'I told you that I didn't want any more wine.'

He shrugged. 'You may change your mind later on. I've a distinct feeling that you will. Now I'm willing to forget this unnecessary quarrel. I suggest that you do the same.'

Enraged by his complacency, she got to her feet and went straight to the bathroom. For a moment she stood, trembling, looking at her reflection in the mirror, then she turned on the cold water and splashed her face. How was it possible that she could ever have thought she was in love with a man like him? she asked herself. Had it been a subconscious way of submerging her guilt? After all, that was the best excuse of all for having sex, wasn't it? You simply convinced yourself that you were in love with the man and that made everything all right.

When she went back into the bedroom five minutes later she saw that the wine had arrived and she scowled at him. She had one last desperate card to play and she tried it now. 'I've just been sick,' she lied. 'I think I'm pregnant.' She lowered her eyes in embarrassment. 'It looks as if you've done what you intended. There's nothing to stop you using the phone now.'

He looked at her thoughtfully. 'I see... You're quite sure about it?'

'Yes. Positive. I've never suffered from sickness before.'

He nodded. 'Very well.' He reached for the phone then paused. 'If I order the release of your brother will you sleep with me tonight? Just one last time?'

Her breath caught in her throat. 'No! I...I...' Her voice trailed away in confusion as she felt the power of those green eyes awakening the slumbering demon in her soul. She looked from him to the bed then back again and bit her lip.

'Why not, Carrie?' he coaxed softly. 'It's not too much to ask, is it? Your brother's freedom in exchange for one last night in my arms. You surely can't detest me that much, can you?'

She closed her eyes and nodded once. 'All...all right. I'll do it.'

'Yes. I thought you would.'

Something about the tone of his voice jerked her eyes open and her heart sank when she saw the sardonic tilt to his mouth. 'Do you take me for a complete idiot?' he asked mockingly. 'You can't possibly tell if you're pregnant yet. It's too early. Now let's have a drink and stop all this foolishness.'

She dug her nails into her palms until the pain overcame her rage then she took a deep breath and said quietly, 'You're a despicable excuse for a man.'

'You didn't think so last night.'

'I didn't see you in your true colours last night,' she countered.

'You only see what you want to see,' he replied, equally blunt. 'That's the trouble with being an idealist. Now the next time you come to me and tell me that you're pregnant you'd better be pretty damned sure that you are because you're going to have to submit to a pregnancy test before I'm satisfied.' Ignoring the look of outrage on her face, he went on, 'The test will be carried out by our own family doctor. The same doctor, incidentally, who confirmed my sister's pregnancy.'

He poured two glasses of wine then said casually, 'If he finds that you aren't pregnant then we start all over again. Personally, I don't care how long it takes. Now do you want this drink or not?'

She ignored his outstretched hand and sank weakly on to the settee. This nightmare was getting worse by the minute. There had to be some way out. Something she could do. Pleading and begging was out of the question, not because of pride—she was long past that stage by now—but because she knew that it would not have the slightest effect on him.

She stared dismally at the carpet for a moment then she got slowly to her feet and confronted him calmly. 'Very well, Nikos. I'll have your child and pray that it's a boy. A boy as strong and sure of himself as you are.'

'Good. I'm sure he will be.'

She gave him a cold smile. 'Yes. So am I. Because as soon as he's old enough to understand I'm going to tell him what you did. I'll tell him how his own father deserted him and me, his mother. He'll hate you, Nikos. And I'll feed that hatred every single day until he reaches manhood. And when that day comes he'll seek you out and destroy you and your whole rotten clan.'

The silence in the room grew taut as he stared at her resolute face. Finally he smiled. 'Don't you think you're being a bit melodramatic, Carrie? After all, it may be a girl. And in any case who knows where any of us will be in twenty years' time?' He shook his head. 'No, Carrie. A threat like that doesn't impress me one little bit. You'll have to do better than that.' He thrust the glass at her again. 'Now take this. You look as if you need it.'

Well, that was it, she thought bleakly. She was out of ammunition now and tooth and nail were no use against this man's impervious shell of self-assurance. Hardly aware of what she was doing, she took the glass and swallowed the contents in one go.

'That's better,' he said in approval. 'Now, shall we settle down and watch some TV before we go to bed or would you rather go out to a nightclub?'

She eyed him bitterly. 'If your sister is anything like you are then God knows what Jimmy saw in her.'

'Her looks and figure, I should imagine. Like all the Spirakis women Helen is extremely beautiful.'

'Yes . . .' she muttered darkly. 'And I'll bet they all know their place, don't they? They must be a miserable bunch of poor downtrodden wretches if all the Spirakis men are like you. I don't know what you've got in your veins. It isn't blood—more like cold acid.'

He laughed harshly at her observation and refilled her glass. 'I happen to be more liberal-minded than my brothers and cousins. It's only thanks to my intervention that your brother is still alive. They were all for taking direct and drastic action but I managed to persuade them that this way was more fitting.' He refilled his own glass and raised it mockingly. 'Here's to your brother's continued good health.'

Her eyes searched his face and she asked quietly, 'Don't you feel the least twinge of guilt about the way you're treating me? I'm a woman just like the sister you care so much about.'

For the briefest of moments there was something in his eyes—something tense and pained—then it was gone and the hard, uncompromising glint was back. 'I have no option. I'm the eldest son and the other members of the family expect me to avenge this insult to their honour. It's my duty.'

'Your duty?' She shot him a look of contempt. 'That's probably what the Roman emperors said when they threw the Christians to the lions.'

'Yes,' he agreed drily. 'They probably did.'

She drained her glass and handed it back. 'Fill it up.'

'That's two glasses you've drunk within two minutes,' he warned.

'Fill the damn thing up or I'll do it myself,' she said tiredly.

He obliged then she pushed her way past him and took the drink out on to the balcony. In the quiet street below she could see couples strolling arm in arm, hear the hum of conversation and the sound of light laughter in the night air. Just ordinary people out enjoying their lives. She wondered if they knew how lucky they were.

Nikos's description of his bloodthirsty relatives had just added to her worries. Jimmy was a free spirit like herself and he wouldn't be taking any form of incarceration without causing as much trouble as he could. Suppose they became impatient and decided that their way was better after all? She shuddered at the thought. First thing in the morning she was going to demand to speak to her brother over the phone.

Meanwhile she was going to have to concede defeat and let Genghis Khan do his worst to her. Finishing her third glass of wine, she went back inside.

Ignoring him, she made straight for the bottle and refilled her glass right to the brim. 'I want to talk to Jimmy first thing in the morning,' she said over her shoulder.

'Why?' he drawled. 'Are you thinking of castigating him for all the trouble he's caused?'

'I want to make sure that he's still in one piece, that's why.'

'You have my word for that.'

She whirled on him. 'I want to hear it from his own lips, damn you. Are you so bloody-minded and uncaring that you won't even let me talk to my own brother?'

He shrugged nonchalantly. 'All right. Calm down. I'll arrange it.'

She glowered at him. 'You'd better.'

He watched her drain her glass and fill it again. 'Are you trying to get yourself drunk? You're going the right way about it. That wine is strong.'

The room seemed to sway a little and she hiccuped. 'The stronger the better.' She pointed to the bed. 'Before I get in there with you I'm going to get revoltingly, disgustingly drunk. Then just at the peak of your... your performance I'm going to be sick all over you.' She raised the glass to her lips again then paused and focused her eyes on him. 'With any luck it'll put you off sex for the rest of your life.'

'Put that glass down,' he said with quiet menace. 'Not only are you making a fool of yourself but you're going to wake up with one gigantic hangover.'

She affected a look of horror. 'A hangover! Oh, my goodness! I mustn't get a hangover, must I? That would be awful!' She paused and hiccuped again before glaring at him. 'You cretin! It doesn't matter if I wake up with a little stranger inside me sharing my life-support system, I suppose. Do you think I'm worried about having a hangover?' Defiantly she raised her glass and swallowed the contents.

'Well, that's the first bottle gone,' he remarked drily. 'Only one left. Shall I order a caseful?'

'Yes,' she slurred. 'Why not? Let's have a bloody party to celebrate while we're at it.' She looked at him hazily. 'It's not your birthday or anything, is it? No? Nor mine. Doesn't matter. I'll think of something. Now let's see...I know! The very thing. We'll call it a conception party!' Pleased at her own brilliance, she was attempting to remove the cork from the second bottle when he snatched it from her.

'You've had enough,' he growled. 'Now get undressed.'

The room began swaying again and he grabbed her shoulders. Staring up mockingly into his green eyes, she scolded him, 'Wassa matter? Getting impatient, are we?'

'Angry would be a better description,' he said heavily. 'Now get undressed or I'll do it for you.'

'Oh, no, you won't!' Somehow she managed to push him away without falling over. 'I'm prefekly cipa . . . capib . . . I can do it myself, thank you very much.' She found the top button of her blouse and was about to undo it when she stopped and raised indignant eyebrows at him. 'You're not just going to stand there watching me, are you? Can't you at least turn your back? I'm not going to run away.'

For a tense moment he looked as if he was ready to bite her head off then he gave a sigh of exasperation and turned away.

'That's much better,' she mumbled. 'I know it's an effort for a man like you but you can be a gennelman if you try.'

It took her longer than usual but she finally managed to unbutton her blouse. The skirt was no problem but she couldn't reach the clip on her bra.

If only the damned floor would stay still for a moment. Finally she gave up the unequal struggle and tapped him on the shoulder. 'Excuse me.'

He turned and she blinked up at him apologetically. 'I'm sorry. I can't seem to be able to reach the clip on my bra. Do you think you could...?'

His arms reached round her in a loose embrace and his fingers deftly undid the hook and eye. Her bra fluttered to the floor as she shrugged her shoulders and she said with stiff formality, 'Thank you. You may let me go now.'

He looked down at the rich, inviting flesh then growled deep in his throat, 'I don't think that would be a good idea. You look ready to pass out.' Before she knew what was happening he'd swept her off her feet and laid her gently on the bed.

For a moment she lay quietly staring up at him and for some strange reason she felt a hard lump in her throat and her lip began to tremble. Then in a small vulnerable voice she said, 'I wouldn't care. If only I thought that you cared about me just a little I wouldn't mind. Honestly, Nikos, I wouldn't.'

Biting her lip, she closed her eyes and waited...

CHAPTER SEVEN

THE morning banged a dustbin lid on her head and told her to wake up. Carrie opened her eyes a fraction then screwed them shut again and moaned. She tried again a moment later and this time managed to keep them open as she blinked at the ceiling.

Last night! Oh, my God! She felt like crawling under the sheet again and hiding. Painfully she eased herself up to a sitting position and looked around the hotel room. There was no sign of Nikos but she could hear the water running in the bathroom.

Her temples were throbbing and her tongue felt like an old sock. She'd never felt as bad as this in her life. Did heavy drinkers feel like this every morning? They had to be mad. But surely she hadn't drunk that much? She tried to reconstruct the events of the previous night. There'd been lots of arguing . . . yes . . . she'd told Nikos exactly what she thought of him . . . then what? He'd undressed her? Or had she undressed herself? She wasn't sure about that bit but she remembered him picking her up and laying her on the bed . . .

'Good morning, Carrie.'

He'd just come out of the bathroom, freshly shaved, showered and dressed, and he came over and sat on the edge of the bed. He examined her critically. 'How do you feel?'

She unstuck her tongue and said thickly, 'Fine. Just fine.'

'Well, you don't look fine to me,' he remarked drily. 'You look like the only survivor of a gruesome train wreck.'

'You certainly know how to boost a person's self-confidence, don't you?' she remarked sourly.

'Well, you shouldn't have drunk so much,' he said unsympathetically. 'I warned you about that wine but you wouldn't listen.'

He sat looking at her for a moment then she remembered to pull up the sheet and cover herself.

He got to his feet. 'I've already eaten. How about you? Shall I have something sent up? Bacon and eggs?'

She swallowed and waited till her stomach had calmed down. He'd said that deliberately, the sadist. 'No, thanks. Just strong, sweet coffee. Lots of it.'

He went over to the phone and gave the order to Room Service then came back and sat beside her again. 'Whenever you feel up to it I'll put a call through to the estate.'

She frowned at him. 'Estate?'

'You asked if you could speak to your brother this morning. Don't you remember?'

She nodded then winced at the pain. 'Yes. I . . . I remember that.'

Under the inquisitorial scrutiny of his green eyes she began to feel distinctly uncomfortable.

'What else do you remember?' he asked.

'I'd rather not think about it right now, if you don't mind,' she muttered. Little flashes of memory were already tormenting her. She looked at the un-creased pillow on the other side of the bed and she looked at him in embarrassment. 'Did we . . . I mean . . . did I . . .?'

'No, we didn't,' he snapped with a hard edge of anger. 'You were unconscious. I'm well aware of your opinion of me but I haven't sunk to that level yet.'

He continued to roast her under a glare of injured dignity then, satisfied that she looked suitably chastened, he said, 'You fell asleep almost as soon as I put you to bed. I made sure that you were comfortable then I went out for a couple of hours. When I came back you were snoring like a drunken sailor.' He made a gesture at the chair. 'I spent a damned uncomfortable night on that.'

She saw that her clothes were neatly folded on the dressing-table. 'I . . . I suppose I should thank you.'

'For what? Looking after you? Not taking advantage of your condition?'

She bit her lip miserably. 'You know what I mean. Don't make it any more difficult for me. I feel bad enough already.'

His expression softened a little. 'Last night you called me a bloody-minded, uncaring cretin. Perhaps I just wanted the satisfaction of watching you eating your words this morning.'

She looked towards the bathroom. 'I'd like to go for a shower.'

'A very good idea. Your coffee should be here by the time you're finished.' He rose and diplomatically went over to gaze out of the window as she crept out of bed, grabbed her clothes and made her way to the bathroom.

She revelled under a steaming-hot shower then turned the tap until it was icy cold. Gasping and taking in great gulps of air, she suffered it for a minute then turned the hot on again. Finishing with another icy shower, she stepped out and briskly towelled herself dry. In the toilet cabinet she found some throw-away toothbrushes in little plastic covers and tiny tubes of toothpaste. She scrubbed her teeth clean then rinsed her mouth. Finally she dressed herself then stepped, pink and glowing, into the bedroom.

Nikos poured her a coffee and looked her up and down with approval. 'Now you look much better. Headache gone?'

She nodded and sipped the sweet coffee. 'What time is it?'

He glanced at his watch. 'Almost nine. Why? Are you in a rush to get somewhere?'

'Yes. The market for fresh vegetables. All the best stuff will be gone if I leave it too late.'

He picked up the phone, asked for the manager then said briskly, 'Spirakis here. I want you to send someone from the kitchen down to the market. They've to pick up supplies and take them to a boat in the harbour called the *Miranda*.' He passed her the phone. 'Give him a list of the supplies you need.'

So that was how the rich and powerful did it, she told herself wryly. They didn't stand around haggling in a market—they got someone from the kitchen to do it for them.

As soon as she'd finished dictating her order he asked the hotel switchboard to put him through to a mainland number. She took another sip of her coffee and saw the impatient look on his face as he waited. He glanced at her and said, 'I'm trying to get through to the estate. You're getting the chance to talk to that brother of yours. No long speeches, please. Just make it as short as possible.'

She laid her coffee down and got ready to grab the phone. She had no idea of what she was going to say apart from telling him not to worry but, knowing Jimmy, he'd be more worried about her than about himself. But just to hear each other's voices would give them both a boost.

After another interminable wait he growled into the mouthpiece at the operator, 'Are you sure you're dialling the right number?' Finally he put the phone down in disgust. 'There's no answer.'

She eyed him suspiciously, wondering if this was another one of his tricks to hurt and confuse her, then she decided that his look of mystified impatience was genuine enough.

'Perhaps there's no one in at the moment,' she suggested.

'There's a staff of eight in the main house,' he said irritably. 'At least one of them should be on hand to answer the phone.'

She picked up her coffee again, her downturned mouth registering her disappointment. 'There may be a fault in the line,' she said, offering another suggestion. 'Or at the exchange. Try again in ten minutes' time.'

'I will,' he said grimly. 'But I've a feeling that something is wrong.'

'Wrong?' She went cold. The cup trembled in her hand and she put it down quickly. 'What do you mean, wrong? Can it have anything to do with my brother?' Her voice began to shake. 'I...I warn you, Nikos. If any of your family have harmed him...'

'Your brother is perfectly safe,' he snapped.

'How do you know?' she demanded. 'How can you possibly know? From what you've told me about those vindictive pigs you're related to——'

His eyes flashed at her dangerously then he growled. 'No one would dare disobey my orders.'

His words, in spite of their vehemence, did little to reassure her, and once again the injustice of the whole thing brought a lump of bitterness to her throat. 'I suppose you've got him chained up in some cellar like an animal,' she said in cold accusation. 'That would be your idea of keeping him safe, wouldn't it?'

'Well, it would certainly fit comfortably into your perception of me as a callous brute,' he said with biting sarcasm. 'The fact is that he's probably a lot more comfortable on the estate than he ever was on the *Miranda*. He has a room behind the servants' quarters and he eats the same food as everyone else. He works in the olive groves from seven in the morning until midday. After that his time is his own.'

She found that hard to believe. 'If you allowed him to do as he likes he would have escaped long ago,' she asserted.

'He can do as he likes within reason,' Nikos amended curtly. 'He isn't allowed to go near the main house and naturally he is guarded at all times,'

'By some hairy thug with a shotgun, I suppose?' she sneered.

His eyes grew hard again. 'My cousin Theo would take great exception to that description. He is very fastidious about his appearance.'

'To hell with your cousin Theo,' she muttered.

He shrugged. 'He'll probably end up there sooner or later like the rest of us. However, since we've got a few minutes to spare, there's something else I'd like to discuss with you.'

She sipped her coffee and eyed him suspiciously over the rim. 'Discuss? That makes a change. Up until now you've never even bothered to——'

'For God's sake, woman!' he bristled. 'Can't you sweeten that tongue of yours for five minutes? I stood enough of your insults last night. I'm trying to be reasonable with you but you're not giving me a chance.'

She almost wilted under his fierce glare and hastily put the cup down again. 'All right. I . . . I'm listening.'

His look of resentful impatience lingered on her a moment longer then he walked over to the window and gazed down into the street. 'I've been giving some thought to the future of our child.'

Her heart gave a tiny lurch. This was the first time he'd ever referred to the child as theirs. It wasn't going to be hers or his. It was going to be theirs.

'It isn't right that the innocent should suffer for the sins of someone else,' he declared quietly.

She was in total agreement with that but to hear such a sentiment coming from him was the last thing she expected. Unable to think of a thing to say, she waited for him to show any other signs of a sudden conversion.

He turned round slowly and scowled at her. 'You made a threat last night about bringing up our child to hate me for deserting both of you. Do you remember that?'

She swallowed uncomfortably. 'V-vaguely. I don't think I meant it.'

'Well, I happen to think that you did,' he said brusquely. 'But that doesn't intimidate me. If I decide to be generous with you now it has nothing to do with that threat. I want you to understand that, Carrie. No one threatens Nikos Spirakis.'

'I see . . .' She bit her lip again. 'Just what do you mean by being generous with me? I mean, at the risk of making you blow your top again I'll tell you right here and now what you can do with any offer of money you might be thinking of making. If and when I do have your child I'll bring it up without any help from you.'

He gave her a long, hard, penetrating look which she returned unflinchingly. 'I should have remembered your stubborn streak of independence,' he murmured.

'You're right,' she retorted. 'I am independent. But apart from that I've no intention of letting you whitewash your conscience by accepting your money.'

His face was an unreadable mask and she wondered what was really at the back of his mind. Was it possible that he was starting to feel . . .? No. That would still be too much to hope for. She decided to push him a little further. 'You've just said that it isn't right that the innocent should suffer because of the sins of someone else. Well, what about me?'

He frowned. 'You won't suffer. When your time comes you'll get the best possible medical attention. You'll want for nothing.'

'And where will I be when all this is happening?' she challenged. 'In the loving bosom of your family?'

He shook his head. 'You know that's impossible.'

'Yes.' She felt that lump come back to her throat. 'I just wanted to hear you say it.'

'You can have a private ward in the best——'

She cut him short. 'No, thanks, Nikos.'

Anger and puzzlement darkened his features. 'Why not?'

Her voice was a mixture of sorrow and resentment as she gave her answer to that. 'If you have to ask then you'll never understand.'

She knew the risk she was running. Obviously he was having some kind of change of heart and finding it heavy going. If she kept rejecting these tentative offers of friendship he might decide just to climb back into his tank.

'If you really want to be generous with me then there is one thing you can do,' she offered quietly.

He nodded gravely. 'Just tell me.'

She took a deep breath. He'd probably turn her down flat but she had at least to try for Jimmy's sake. 'Let my brother go. Turn him free.' She saw his eyes narrow and she went on quickly, 'You don't need him as a hostage any more, Nikos. That was why you took him in the first place, wasn't it? Just to make sure that I'd . . . I'd co-operate with you. Well, I have . . .'

She saw the cold refusal on his face even before he managed to open his mouth and she got her argument in first. 'Look, I'm willing to stay with you until...until your own doctor examines me. That's what you want, isn't it?'

His frown of indecision told her that he was thinking about it and she scented a small victory. 'Jimmy has friends in Piraeus,' she went on persuasively. 'He can stay with them for a few weeks.'

'You'll entertain no notion of escaping?'

'I've already told you that I'll stay,' she reminded him stiffly. 'You'll just have to take my word for it.'

His green eyes contemplated her briefly then he nodded. 'Very well. I agree.'

As the great weight was suddenly lifted from her shoulders she felt as if her feet were leaving the ground and her breath came out in a long sigh of relief.

'And the other matter?' he asked quietly. 'Do you still refuse to accept my help with the child?'

Watch it, Carrie, she thought. Don't blow it now. She'd already wrung one concession from him and it would be silly to jeapordise it now. If she went out of her way to antagonise him he might just change his mind about Jimmy. 'I...I'll think about it,' she prevaricated. 'When the time comes I may well be needing some kind of help.'

It was enough to keep him satisfied for the moment and he went back to the phone and asked the operator to try the number again. She poured herself another cup of coffee and watched him.

Still unable to get any reply from the estate, he replaced the phone and stared out of the window with a dark, brooding expression.

Prudently she kept her mouth shut. She knew to her cost what happened when his train of thought was interrupted by 'small talk'. Yesterday morning on the *Miranda* she'd tried it and had received a very cold shoulder. Was that when he'd begun thinking about the future of their child? she wondered.

He came to a sudden decision and turned. 'Finish your coffee. We're leaving. It should be little more than a seven-hour trip to the mainland from here. We can be at the estate by this evening if we leave right away.'

She looked at him hesitantly. Going into the heart of enemy territory was not a prospect that pleased her.

'You'd like to see your brother before I release him and send him on his way, wouldn't you?' he asked drily. 'This is your chance. In any case I have to find out why there is no answer to my call. A few heads will roll when I get to the bottom of this. All our enterprises are run from the estate and success depends on instant communication.'

The *Miranda* slipped out of the harbour half an hour later. Nikos took the wheel while she inspected the provisions which had arrived a few minutes before they'd left. After she'd stowed them in the galley she came back up on deck and stripped to the waist. It was strange how she'd never have dreamt of doing this in front of her own brother yet in full view of Nikos she didn't feel the slightest bit embarrassed. She sat on the deck with her back to the wheelhouse and basked in the sun. Half an hour would be long enough to maintain her light golden tan then she'd don her T-shirt. The Aegean during August was no place to take chances with sunburn . . . or anything worse.

Now that the problem of her brother's safety was out of the way she had time to weigh up her own situation. There was no use dwelling on the rights and wrongs of it, because in approximately nine months' time she was going to have a baby, so the sooner she started making plans the better.

The first thing to do was to stop feeling sorry for herself. It wasn't the end of the world. She wouldn't be the first woman in history to find herself in this position. She'd manage somehow. Women were more resilient and adaptable than men.

Of one thing she was certain. She'd raise the child with all the tender loving care she was capable of. At the end of the day her baby would be the most innocent of them all. Anyway, she'd have to find a permanent home somewhere, and perhaps a job. Handling a boat wasn't the only thing she could do. She still had her business studies diploma to fall back on. There were plenty of shipping agencies in Piraeus. She might get lucky there.

She wasn't so sure about her brother, though. She'd have to make it perfectly clear that she held him in no way responsible. He'd been stupid and thoughtless, but then most men usually were, weren't they? Show them a big bust and a pair of pretty legs and they went ga-ga. But Jimmy wouldn't see it that way. Every time he saw the child it would be a reminder of his folly and he'd be driven half mad with shame and remorse. The best thing all round would be for Jimmy to find a new partner to help him run the *Miranda*. That way they could go their separate ways.

In a strange twist of logic she even found herself feeling a little sorry for Nikos. He was going to be the father of a child which he was destined never to see. That was a fact that he apparently hadn't considered up till now and it was probably the reason for his belated offer of help. If she kept refusing him then she was virtually denying him the right ever to see his offspring.

Did she really want to do that? she asked herself. She hated what he was doing to her life but she couldn't really bring herself to hate him as a person. He wasn't an evil man. Their respective cultures were a world apart but if she was to be truly honest with herself she'd have to admit that she'd been a willing partner in her own seduction. If she'd met him in any other circumstances she'd probably still have fallen for his raw masculine sex appeal and she'd still have been left to pay the price. In that respect there wasn't much to choose between her and her brother.

When her half-hour was up she put on her T-shirt and went below. In the galley she made a plateful of tomato and cucumber sandwiches then took a jugful of ice-cold orange juice from the fridge and carried the tray to the wheelhouse.

'Help yourself,' she said. 'I'll take a spell at the wheel.'

Handing control over to her, he poured himself some orange juice then warned her, 'Keep your eye on those yachts ahead. They're tacking into the wind so they're liable to cut across your bows when you least expect it.'

She sighed and rolled her eyes upwards. He laughed at her expression then conceded, 'Sorry. I forgot that you were an old sea dog.'

There was a slight swell which the *Miranda* was riding easily and the breeze was mercifully cooling. Nikos was chewing at a sandwich but he stopped abruptly when she asked him about his sister.

'Helen? What about her?'

She shrugged. 'I'm just wondering what she's like. After all, she and I are in much the same position, aren't we? I suppose we've got that much in common.'

Nikos finished chewing then swallowed and said, 'You may get the chance to meet her. Curiosity might make her want to meet the sister of the man who abused her.'

She flinched at his choice of words then responded sarcastically, 'You mean she's still living there?'

'Of course. Why shouldn't she?'

'Well, the way you were talking about her I thought she'd been packed off in disgrace to live with some old aunt in the mountains. I'm sure she's grateful not to be completely ostracised from her loving, caring family.'

Ignoring the sarcasm, Nikos took another bite of his sandwich. 'She'll be leaving for America any day now. It's more convenient to let her remain in the house. Naturally she's confined to her own suite with her personal maid. Not as a punishment, you understand. More to save her embarrassment in front of other members of the family.'

'She's been sent to Coventry, in other words?'

He frowned. 'Sent to Coventry?'

'Sorry. It's an English expression. It means that she's not the flavour of the month at your household.'

Again he looked puzzled. 'Flavour of the month?'

She sighed. 'Forget it. Anyway, you still haven't told me what she's like as a person. I mean, I realise that she must be very beautiful but she must have other qualities besides.' She paused then goaded him into answering by adding casually, 'If you don't want to talk about her that's all right by me. I'll understand. After the shame she's brought on you all...' She stopped and hoped she hadn't gone too far.

She could sense him stiffening then he drawled, 'She's a bit like yourself, Carrie. Resourceful and courageous but with too much salt on her tongue for her own good.'

She stared straight ahead, afraid to let him see the hurt and confusion in her eyes. A lot of good it did being courageous and resourceful when you ended up like this, she thought. 'Is she also an idealist... a romantic dreamer like me?' she asked quietly.

'Yes. And like you she's sensible enough to know that in the end it's best to bow to the inevitable.' He paused for a moment then went on darkly, 'And you're right about her bringing shame to our family. She is as much to blame as your brother for allowing it to happen. She now realises the error of her ways and is——'

Carrie couldn't take it any more and she wished she'd never got on to the subject in the first place. Turning to him sharply, she said, 'All right, Nikos!

I don't want to hear any more. I'm depressed enough as it is.'

'Then we'll have to try our best to lift that depression,' he mocked softly. 'There's a secluded villa on the estate. We'll spend the night together there and this time there'll be no wine to dull the senses.' He leaned over and his lips brushed warmly against her ear. 'Just keep thinking about that for the next few hours, Carrie. Imagine the pleasure we're going to give one another.'

She eyed him resentfully as he left the wheelhouse then she bit her lip. Pleasure was the last thing on her mind right now. Top of the list was still her brother and what she was going to say to him when they met.

He was going to demand to know everything that Nikos had done to her. Well, she could lie and talk her way out of that just to put his mind at rest but how was she going to explain about her promise to stay with Nikos? If she told Jimmy the truth he'd go berserk. That would have to wait until later when they were both safely out of the clutches of the Spirakis family. In the meantime she'd have to try and think up some plausible story explaining why she couldn't leave with him.

From a mile offshore she could see the full extent of the estate. The harbour they were heading for was large enough to accommodate a fair-sized fleet of ships. Through the binoculars she counted at least twenty, ranging from a magnificent luxury cruiser to large yachts and smaller power boats. Fronting the harbour were various sheds and workshops and beyond them, on the gently rising ground, the main house itself fronted by immaculate lawns and flowerbeds. Behind the house, stretching as far as the foothills in the distance, were vast acres of olive groves and fruit orchards.

The *Miranda*, looking like a bag lady at a débutantes' ball, nosed her way through the harbour towards the jetty. Nikos guided her safely to a berth and from the deck she threw a stern line up to the jetty where it was grabbed by a worker and tied to a bollard. As she was doing the same to the bow line a white limousine screeched to a halt and two men leapt out, one demanding to know in a loud voice just who the hell she was and who had given her permission to tie up on private property.

Suddenly their expressions changed as Nikos stepped out of the wheelhouse and she saw them exchange uneasy glances.

Nikos, wasting no time, climbed on to the jetty and confronted them angrily. 'We wouldn't have to be here at all if I'd been able to get an answer to my phone call this morning. I hope for both your sakes there's a damned good explanation.'

Again they looked at each other in embarrassment then the elder of the two, a burly man in his late fifties, drew Nikos aside and began talking in a low, urgent whisper.

Carrie became aware of the other man staring down at her. He was about the same age as herself, smartly dressed in a dark suit, but his lips were too thick and his eyes almost colourless. For a moment she glared back at him defiantly then she turned her back on him and pretended to be busy inspecting the derrick. There was something about him that made her skin crawl. The sooner she saw Jimmy and got away from here the better, she decided.

With a feeling of relief she saw Nikos return to the deck. Better the devil you knew than the one you didn't, she told herself wryly. But the feeling of relief vanished as soon as she saw the look of fury on his face and she gulped, 'Wh-what's wrong, Nikos?'

In a voice of barely controlled anger he said, 'It seems that there's a very good reason why no one was in the house to answer the phone this morning. Everyone was out searching for your brother.'

Her eyes widened. 'Jimmy? I . . . I don't understand. Where is he?'

'That's what we'd all like to know. He's disappeared.'

'You mean he's escaped?' She felt like giving a small smile of triumph but thought better of it. He didn't look as if he'd appreciate any snide remarks from her. She gave a shrug. 'I don't see why you're so upset. You were going to let him go anyway, weren't you? He's just beaten you to it, that's all.' She could still feel those colourless eyes staring down at her and she said quietly, 'Look, Nikos. I don't like your friend up there, whoever he is. Since there's no reason for us to be here any longer, why don't we just start the engine and——?'

'That man you've taken an irrational dislike to is my cousin Theo.'

The name rang a bell and she smiled coldly. 'He's the one who was supposed to be guarding Jimmy, isn't he? Seems he's not very good at his job.'

'During the night your brother pretended to be ill and when Theo went to his assistance he was overpowered, tied up and gagged. He didn't manage to free himself until seven o'clock this morning.'

This time she couldn't help herself. 'Well, that's Jimmy for you. He always was good at knots. Dad taught him well.'

For a moment she thought she'd gone too far and that Nikos was going to strike her and she backed away.

His green eyes flickered angrily then he took a deep breath. 'You won't find the next part so humorous, Carrie. Not content with merely making his escape, he has also abducted my sister.'

Her mouth dropped open. 'From this house? How did he manage that?'

'Made his way to her room then tied her up and gagged her as he did to Theo, I imagine.' He smiled at her grimly. 'No doubt his idea is to use Helen as a hostage in exchange for you. We'll find him, and when we do...'

He left the threat unfinished and she closed her eyes in despair. In spite of everything she'd done her damn fool of a brother had just got himself into more trouble than ever.

CHAPTER EIGHT

CARRIE tried her best to ignore the looks she was getting but it wasn't easy. There was an atmosphere of brooding hostility in the room that made her decidedly nervous. Nikos had spent a good ten minutes questioning and tongue-lashing the staff and members of the family and you could see who they were blaming for their troubles. Her. It was all her fault. If they couldn't take their wrath out on Jimmy she was the next best thing.

Finally Nikos dismissed them all in disgust and as they shuffled out of the room he called one of them back.

The girl was about nineteen, dark and slim, and could have been quite pretty except for the surly expression on her face. 'Yes, Mr Spirakis?'

Nikos spoke to her gravely. 'Sofia, this is Carrie. She is the sister of the man who has abducted your mistress. In spite of that you will treat her with the same respect and consideration you gave to Helen. I'd intended to put her up in the villa but in the circumstances I think it would be more convenient if she was given a room in the main house.'

The maid nodded and said with stiff formality, 'I'll see to it, Mr Spirakis. How long will our guest be staying with us?'

'At least a month.' He fixed his green eyes on Carrie as if expecting an argument, then he smiled thinly. 'We still have some unfinished business to attend to, don't we, Carrie? It's now more important than ever that it's brought to a final and satisfying conclusion. I think you'll agree, Carrie.'

'Have I any option?' she asked resignedly. 'I've no doubt you've something nasty in mind as usual for Jimmy unless I do. We're back to square one again, aren't we?'

'Yes. It appears so, thanks to your brother's stupidity. However, we can discuss your future more comfortably over dinner this evening.'

Dejectedly she followed the maid out of the room. About the only crumb of comfort she could think of was Nikos's instruction that she was to be treated with respect and consideration. Well, she'd just have to wait and see but, judging from the frosty expression on the maid's face, the prospects looked bleak. Apart from Nikos everyone she'd seen so far had looked as if they'd like nothing more than to hang her up by her thumbs.

The house had seemed large from the outside but inside it seemed even larger. She'd need a map to find her way around here, she thought. Or maybe she'd be kept under lock and key with a guard at the door as they'd done with Jimmy.

At last she found herself being ushered into a large, comfortably furnished bedroom and as soon as they were both inside the maid shut the door firmly behind her then heaved a huge sigh of relief. 'It's safe now. No one can hear us in here.'

She blinked at the maid. 'Pardon?'

'Sofia. Please call me Sofia, Carrie. I'm your friend. The only one you have here.' Miraculously the surly expression had been replaced by a conspiratorial yet friendly smile. She gestured round the room. 'Will this suit you? There are plenty more to choose from.'

Feeling slightly bewildered, Carrie muttered, 'It's very nice.' She frowned at the maid. 'Look, Sofia . . . what did you mean about not being heard?'

The maid snorted. 'The less they know the better.'

'Know about what? And who are they?'

'All of them,' the maid said enigmatically. 'Don't trust them. Any of them. They'll trick you into telling them what they want to know.' She changed the subject quickly. 'Where are your things?'

This was getting unreal, thought Carrie. 'What things?'

'Your cases? Your clothes?'

'I don't have any. Just clean jeans and T-shirts aboard the boat.'

Sofia frowned. 'You can't have dinner with Nikos if you're wearing jeans,' she protested. She opened the door, peered outside, then beckoned. 'Follow me. We'll find you something really beautiful to wear.'

Carrie hesitated then sighed. No doubt she'd get to the bottom of this behaviour sooner or later. She followed the maid along a corridor until they came to a massive oak door. Sofia pulled a key from around her neck and inserted it in the lock.

When they were inside, she was led into a smaller room off the main one and Sofia slid aside a huge mirrored door to reveal a wardrobe.

Carrie stared at the racks of suits and dresses in awe. Tentatively she touched a shimmering creation in black silk and said, 'You're right. These are beautiful. Whom do they belong to?'

'My, Helen, of course. This is her private suite. She has good taste, yes?'

Carrie withdrew her hand as if she'd been stung. 'Helen's! I can't wear any of her stuff.'

Sofia looked hurt and puzzled. 'Of course you can! You're Jimmy's sister, aren't you? She'd want you to have them.'

'Would she?' It was beginning to dawn on her what the trouble was here. Sofia was assuming that she knew...knew what? Of course! She should have realised right from the start. Taking a deep breath, she said, 'Helen is in love with Jimmy, isn't she?'

The maid blinked at her in astonishment. 'They're mad about each other! Didn't you know?'

Carrie felt like hugging her. 'No, I didn't. But believe me, Sofia, you've lifted a load off my mind. Up till now I've assumed that it was just a casual affair Jimmy had had. I had no idea how serious it was.'

'He didn't tell you? His own sister? He didn't tell you about Helen?' The maid's voice was a gasp of disbelief then she nodded slowly. 'Helen must have forbidden him to tell anyone. Even you. She was afraid of what they'd do to her if they found out.'

Carrie grabbed her hand and pulled her over to the settee. 'I want you to tell me all about it, Sofia. How they met...how long they've known each other.'

Sofia launched herself into the story eagerly. 'Once a week I used to accompany Helen on a shopping trip. She used to look forward to it because it was the only chance she ever got to get away from this house. We'd go shopping and have a meal and Helen loved being able to act like any other girl for a change. Sometimes we went to the beach or the cinema——'

Carrie broke in gently, 'How did she meet my brother?'

'Oh . . . yes. That was about six months ago. Our car had broken down and Jimmy fixed it. Oh, Carrie, if you'd seen the way they looked at each other! I'd never seen Helen so happy. They met every time Jimmy was in port after that. We'd drive into town then I'd leave them and——'

'What happened when she found out that she was pregnant?'

Sofia's face darkened. 'They tricked her into telling who the father was. They said they'd invite him to the house to discuss the wedding arrangements.'

'Nikos did that?' she asked sharply.

Sofia shook her head. 'Nikos was away on business at the time. It was those other pigs. His uncle and his cousins. Helen told them when Jimmy was due back so they waited . . .'

She didn't need to hear the rest. She could guess what they'd told Nikos when he'd returned. They'd engineered the whole thing and while they'd lain in wait for Jimmy Nikos had come to the *Miranda* seeking vengeance.

She was almost afraid to ask the next question but she had to know. 'You say that they're all pigs, Sofia. Does that include Nikos?'

The maid put her head to one side and regarded her thoughtfully then smiled. 'Are you in love with Nikos?'

'No. Of...of course not.' Her denial didn't sound very convincing. Not even to herself.

Sofia kept smiling. 'If you say so. But you needn't worry. Nikos is a hard man but he's honest. And he treats the staff well.'

Carrie tried to tell herself that it didn't matter one way or the other but it did and she felt a little better. 'Look,' she said, 'I don't think that Nikos really knows how much Helen and Jimmy love each other. If we tell him——'

Sofia looked at her in horror. 'No! You can't!'

'But . . . surely he would want his own sister to be happy?' she asked, puzzled.

Sofia gave a bitter laugh. 'You are English so you wouldn't understand about these things. If it was as easy as that don't you think that Helen would have told him herself?'

Carrie sighed. She suspected that Sofia was right. Women here weren't allowed to have minds of their own. They were to be seen but not heard and God help any stranger who came along and tried to steal one.

Sofia laughed suddenly. 'They think that they are so clever but Helen and I fooled them. We helped Jimmy to escape and they still don't suspect a thing.' She glanced at the door as if still afraid of being overheard then went on, 'They were keeping Jimmy in a room in the servants' quarters. The room next to mine, as a matter of fact. The walls there are thin and at night Jimmy and I could whisper to each other and pass messages. He told me of his plan to get out but he needed a rope to tie up the guard. I got that for him.'

Carrie heaved another sigh of relief. 'So it isn't true that he tied and gagged Helen and forced her to go with him?'

Sofia scoffed at the idea. 'Of course not. Helen was already outside waiting for him. They went down to the harbour and stole a boat. As far as I can find out those fools haven't yet discovered that one of their boats is missing. They seem to think that Jimmy made for the main road and managed to steal a car.'

'So where are they now?' Carrie asked breathlessly. 'Do you know?'

Sofia shook her head vigorously. 'I didn't want to know. What I don't know I can't be forced or tricked into telling. But Jimmy said that you'd know where he'd gone.'

Carrie thought for a moment then she smiled. 'Yes. I think I do.'

'Then be careful they don't trick you into telling them,' Sofia warned. She got to her feet and went over to the wardrobe. 'Now then . . . it will be time for dinner soon. We must choose something very special for you.'

They were alone in the dining-room. She had finally decided on a low-cut dress in red silk. It had still been wrapped in tissue paper in the box. Helen had bought it on the spur of the moment, Sofia had told her, but had never had the nerve actually to wear it. Across the candlelit table Nikos looked devastating in a white dinner-jacket.

The meal was delicious. Of that she had no doubt. The trouble was that she'd been too nervous really to appreciate it. They'd eaten in silence and when the servant had taken the last dish away Nikos poured her another glass of wine and smiled thinly. 'You won't get drunk on this stuff, Carrie, so you needn't look so alarmed. It's almost non-alcoholic.'

She took the glass from him and muttered, 'Good. I don't want to wake up with any more raging headaches.'

He raised his own glass to her in a silent toast then remarked, 'That dress suits you. Where did you get it?'

She'd already decided on the lie but it still came uneasily. 'I think it belongs to Sofia. She's been very good to me.'

His eyes narrowed thoughtfully. 'Yes. She's a good girl. She and Helen are very close. More like sisters really. And I've got a feeling that our little Sofia knows more about this affair than she is letting on.'

She affected a look of surprise. 'That's not the impression I got. She's very concerned about Helen. At least she's not blaming me for what happened—unlike some of the other people around here.'

'You've nothing to fear from anyone in this house,' he said grimly. 'You have my personal assurance of that.'

'I'm glad to hear it,' she murmured. She remembered the young one with the colourless eyes. Theo. He'd been slavering at her like a hungry wolf while Nikos had been tearing them off a strip. Even the older one, the uncle, had looked like a snake ready to strike.

Nikos toyed with his glass for a moment. 'There are too many puzzling aspects to this affair. I'm going to get to the bottom of it.'

'How do you mean, puzzling?' she asked innocently. 'I thought you'd made up your mind that it was a straightforward case of kidnapping. Jimmy took Helen and intends exchanging her for me. That's what you told me.'

He gave her a smile completely devoid of humour. 'Your brother overcame the man who was supposed to be guarding him and managed to tie him up. Then he apparently made his way silently and unobserved all the way through the house to Helen's suite. Then he tied her up and gagged her in case she screamed, slung her over his shoulder like an old carpet and walked brazenly out of the front door.' He raised a sceptical eyebrow. 'It's the sort of scene you might see in a very bad B movie. Wouldn't you agree?'

She shrugged. 'So what are you suggesting?'

'I was hoping that you might have some ideas to put forward,' he drawled.

This was exactly what Sofia had warned her about. He suspected Sofia and he suspected that she had confided in Carrie and now he was asking all these casual questions, trying to trick Carrie. 'Why should I know anything about it?' she countered uneasily.

'A woman's instinct?' he asked nonchalantly. 'You should know better than anyone what your brother is capable of.'

'I know that he isn't capable of kidnapping someone,' she said hotly. 'The very idea is ridiculous. He's not that kind of man.'

Nikos stared at her intently. 'Are you suggesting then that Helen went with him willingly?'

She returned his stare with a look of defiance. 'Perhaps she did.' Then she added acidly, 'She's your sister. You should know better than me what *she's* capable of.'

His green eyes continued to interrogate her. 'You wouldn't even like to hazard a guess as to where your brother might have taken her?'

She gave a good imitation of a sigh of exasperation. 'Are you going to sit here quizzing me all night? I've already told you that I don't know anything.'

He went on relentlessly, ignoring her complaint. 'You mentioned that he had friends in Piraeus. Do you think he might have taken Helen there?'

She smiled at him coldly. 'It's possible. Do you want the address? Then you can send one of your trained apes to find out.' That would suit her fine, she thought. If her guess was right then Jimmy hadn't gone anywhere near Piraeus.

He sipped his drink and regarded her thoughtfully while she had to sit there giving the performance of her life in maintaining an air of injured innocence. She was sure he could read her mind and he was going to keep this up until she cracked under the strain. Damn the man! Nothing would have given her greater pleasure than to tell him the truth but the consequences for Sofia would be dire. And would Helen and Jimmy ever forgive her for betraying them? It was up to her now to protect them until they were either out of the country or legally married.

Finally he sighed. 'You told me once that you were a terrible actress, Carrie. Well, you were right. I know you're lying to me. Now if you really want to help your brother you'll give us your full co-operation in finding him. The quicker he's caught the better.'

'I still don't know anything,' she muttered grimly.

'He won't be harmed.'

She gave a snort of derision. 'Do you expect me to believe that after the threats you've made?'

'Forget the threats,' he said irritably. 'They were made in the heat of the moment. All I'm interested in now is the safe return of my sister. This humiliation has gone on long enough.'

Humiliation? So that was it! That was all he was worried about, she told herself bitterly. His injured dignity. The knowledge that once the news leaked out the Spirakis family would be a laughing-stock throughout the country. In a land where macho pride reigned supreme how could they ever again command respect when it was discovered that they couldn't even keep their women in line?

Barely able to contain her anger, she snapped back at him, 'You're very good at dishing out humility but it's a different story when you're on the receiving end, isn't it?' She paused for a moment, calculating the risks, then decided they were worth it, if only to find out his reaction. 'Perhaps your precious sister did leave with my brother of her own accord. For all anyone knows she might even have helped him escape. Perhaps she's in love with him. Have you thought about that? I mean...she is going to have his child, after all.'

His face remained impassive and only the whitening of his knuckles on the glass betrayed his anger. 'Of course I've thought about it. And that's why I want her back before she does something even more foolish.'

'Foolish?' she echoed in disbelief. 'What the hell's foolish about falling in love? It happens all the time. People can't help it. In fact, they like it.'

They glared at each other in silence then he spoke in a flat, calm voice, 'Love is for fools. It's an indulgence that our family can't afford. Helen is a Spirakis and she knows where her duty lies.'

She felt like throwing something at him but contented herself with an abrasive volley of heavy sarcasm. 'Of course! How stupid of me! I was forgetting. She's betrothed to someone else, isn't she? Someone more . . . *acceptable*.' She stressed the last word with contempt.

His dark eyebrows rose a fraction. 'You seem to find that concept strange.'

'I do,' she agreed acridly. 'In fact I find it ridiculous in this day and age. No one should be forced into a marriage.'

'Ah, yes!' His laugh was dry and mocking. 'I too was forgetting. You're the starry-eyed idealist. I should have thought that you'd have learned your lesson by now. Aren't you the one who agreed that it was better to bow to the inevitable?' His tone hardened. 'Power and privilege has its price, Carrie. Helen has always known that. Marriages of convenience are nothing new. Not even in your own country. The English aristocracy have been doing it since the Norman conquest.'

She eyed him in despair then exclaimed, 'For God's sake, Nikos! She's only a kid. She's not a company asset. Do you really expect her to forgo her chance of love and happiness just to consolidate the power of your family? It's . . . it's . . .' She searched for a suitable word to express her outrage, found it then spat it out, 'It's bloody grotesque, that's what it is.'

His displeasure was almost tangible, rolling across the table and swamping her like an icy wave. 'No one here is remotely interested in your opinion. How we regulate our family affairs is our business and no one else's. Our rules have served us well over the years and we don't take kindly to strangers coming here and creating confusion and discord.'

It wasn't so much his anger that dismayed her—she was used enough to that by now—rather it was his unshakeable, rock-solid belief in his own rightness. There was no possible way she could ever pierce that armour of unyielding arrogance.

Sighing with frustration, she scowled at him. 'Even if Helen doesn't like the man you've chosen for her...even then, you'll still force her to go through with it?'

'She has no reason other than wilful stubbornness not to like him,' he asserted with infuriating certainty. 'Ari Palandrous is a well groomed young man from an impeccable background. The son of a well known and influential banker.'

Well, that was that, she thought with a taste of galling defeat. It was a complete waste of time talking to the man and trying to make him change his mind. And then of course all this was very relevant to her own situation. It raised a big question. A very big question. Question *numéro uno* in fact. Their eyes challenged each other over the table then she asked quietly, 'Do these rules apply to the men of the family as well as the women?'

Her eyes searched his face as she waited for his answer. She wasn't sure what she was looking for. A twitch of the mouth? A flash of guilt in the eyes? Some sign of discomfort? But there was nothing. Just blank indifference as he confirmed her fears. 'Yes. We too have our obligations.'

'I see...' Her voice betrayed her with a slight tremble but she got it firmly under control. 'So if by some remote chance you ever do happen to meet someone and...and fall in love you'd just do your best to ignore her, would you?'

His answer was quiet and devoid of any emotion and each word he uttered pierced her heart like a jagged splinter. 'I could never permit myself to fall in love, Carrie. I've already told you, it's an indulgence our family can't afford.'

It was what she'd expected, but to hear him actually say it . . . She steadied her aching heart with a deep breath. 'Well, I suppose that's only fair. I mean . . . you're the head of the family and it's only right that you should set an example.'

He inclined his head; a strange, politely mocking gesture, it seemed to her. 'Good. I'm glad that you finally understand.'

She swallowed painfully. 'Oh, I understand everything now, Nikos. You've made your position perfectly clear to me. And mine. You don't believe in pulling any punches, do you?' She pushed her glass away and dabbed at her lips with her napkin. 'Well, thanks for the meal and the lecture. And now, if you'll excuse me, I'm feeling rather tired.'

He got to his feet, the candlelight arranging his features in yet another forbidding aspect of light and shadow. Only the green eyes remained the same, cold and remote. 'You and I still have an arrangement,' he reminded her quietly. 'As you said, it's back to square one.'

She looked up at him, her dulled eyes suddenly bright with resentment and defiance. 'No. Not any longer, Nikos. Not while my brother is free. You can't harm him now so you've no hold over me.'

'No,' he conceded with a thinly threatening smile. 'But when we do find your brother——'

'*If* you find him, you mean.'

He shrugged. 'He's bound to come back for you, is he not? Or are you telling me that he's prepared to abandon his own sister?'

She got to her feet, all patience gone and re-kindled anger giving her strength as she attempted to push her way past him.

He grabbed her arm. 'Wait. I'll get Sofia to take you back to your room.'

'I'm not going back to my room,' she snarled. 'I'm going to the *Miranda*. I'm leaving here right now. I've had enough of you and your family. You can all roast in hell as far as I'm concerned. Now let go of my arm or I'll scratch your eyes out.'

'You're going nowhere,' he told her with grim certainty. 'You're staying here until I decide otherwise.'

'Then you'll have to lock me up the same way you did Jimmy.'

'I will if necessary,' he warned.

She let out a long explosive breath and glared at him venomously. 'What good do you think it'll do you keeping me here against my will? If you imagine for one minute that I'm ever going to let you take liberties again with my body then you can——'

His angry growl cut her short. 'As for taking liberties with your body, that is entirely up to you, but whether Helen is returned here or not you are still the price your brother has to pay for his mistake.' His hand suddenly reached up and cupped her chin possessively. 'You'll stay here no matter how long that takes so get used to the idea.' Letting her go, he rang a bell, and when the servant appeared he said briskly, 'Send Sofia here. Tell her that Carrie wishes to retire for the night. When you've done that tell Theo to order a guard on board the *Miranda* tonight.'

There was nothing she could do except stand there and stare at him in bleak and bitter frustration. As usual he had the whip hand and it was now obvious that he was getting ready to use it with a vengeance.

When she reached the privacy of the bedroom she sat on the edge of the bed and clenched her fists in total exasperation. Sofia rummaged around in the wardrobe then handed her a flimsy nightdress before breathlessly demanding to know what Nikos had said during the meal.

'Don't worry,' she told the maid tiredly. 'I didn't tell him anything.'

There was a sigh of relief. 'Good. Was . . . was he very angry?'

'Oh, yes,' she said grimly. 'I'd say he was angry.' He'd been lots of other things as well. Arrogant . . . despicable . . . cold . . .

Sofia looked at her uncomfortably. 'Neither Jimmy nor Helen ever thought you'd be involved. What is Nikos going to do now? Is he going to let you go?'

Carrie looked up at the maid's crumpled face and said, 'Don't worry about me, Sofia. I can look after myself.' She hadn't done a very good job of it up till now but things were about to change.

'They . . . they were going to send Helen to America,' Sofia said in quiet outrage. 'She and Jimmy would never have seen one another again. She had to escape with him.'

Carrie took the maid's hand and said gently, 'I know, Sofia, I know. They did the right thing and I'm glad that you helped them.'

'I...I don't suppose I'll ever see them again now,' Sofia whispered brokenly. 'Now that Helen is gone they won't need me around here so I suppose they'll just sack me. I...I don't mind that so much but I'd like to see Helen and Jimmy just once more. To see them together at last and happy.'

Carrie squeezed Sofia's hand in hers. 'I've a feeling that you will. When Jimmy realises that I'm here he'll come and get me.' She bit her lip. 'I just hope that he has the sense to marry Helen before he does.'

Sofia's face brightened. 'Of course! If they are man and wife there's nothing the family can do about it.' She gave an excited laugh. 'Can you imagine the look on their faces if Helen arrived with a wedding-ring on her finger?'

Carrie blinked as the sudden idea flashed into her mind. Why should she wait for Jimmy to come here? That might take long enough. What was to stop her leaving here and going to join him? Nikos had put a guard on the *Miranda* but there were plenty of other boats in the harbour. Faster and more powerful boats. She could steal one. Sofia would help her. Could they do it tonight? she wondered. It was dark and moonless outside.

Caution prevailed. This would have to be planned properly. She'd have to find out what the routine was in the harbour. Choose the right boat and make sure there was enough fuel. It would have to be tomorrow night. She thought about it a little longer, allowing common sense to temper her initial rush of enthusiasm, but the more she thought about it, the more determined she became to thwart the plans of that dark tyrant who treated everyone as pawns on some infernal chessboard of his own devising.

She wondered if she should put the idea to Sofia right now then decided against it. Sofia would probably just lie awake all night full of nervous excitement. She might even do or say something inadvertently that would alert another, less trustworthy member of the staff.

Sofia fussed around for another ten minutes or so, reluctant to leave until Carrie succeeded in assuring her that there was nothing else she needed and that the bed was comfortable enough and that it wasn't too warm and that if she needed her for anything at all during the night she would be sure to ring the bell which was connected to the servants' quarters.

Alone at last, she stripped and donned the sheer silk nightdress then lay down on the bed and stretched over to switch off the bedside lamp. She doubted very much if she'd get any sleep tonight. It was too quiet here and she missed the gentle rocking motion of the *Miranda* and the sound of water lapping and timbers creaking. And then there were the feelings of anger and guilt that kept her mind in a continual turmoil.

In another week's time her biological clock might miss a beat and that would give her the first hint of whether she could be pregnant or not but there was no reason to suppose that the seed of Nikos Spirakis wasn't gestating at this very moment in her womb. There was nothing she could do about it now but it should never have happened in the first place.

She should have guessed that Jimmy would manage to escape sooner or later and she should have waited and given him a fair chance. But no. Not her. How long had it taken her to give in? Six nights, that was all! The night after the storm. That was when she'd surrendered. The night after the storm when she'd foolishly believed that fate had drawn her and Nikos closer together. The night she'd managed to convince herself that he was beginning to respect and like her. Yes. She'd been willing to settle for 'like', hadn't she? Never mind 'love'. 'Like' was good enough. At the time her own driving passion might even have settled for a lot less because deep down she was a fool. Nikos had been right after all. She was an idealist always ready to believe in a happy ending.

Well, there was going to be no happy ending now. Nikos had ruthlessly and brutally blasted all these foolish notions out of her mind. She meant less than the dust on the road to him. Even his own damned sister meant nothing. All he cared about was the spurious honour of the Spirakis name.

It was some time later when she was jerked awake from a fitful doze and she sat up and stared around the darkened room. Had it been a dream or had she really heard voices whispering? No. No dream. There they were again. She switched on the bedside lamp, got out of bed and padded over to the door. 'Who's there?' she called nervously.

The whispering stopped.

'Who's there?' she demanded again in a louder voice. 'What do you want?'

A man's voice answered, thick and heavy. 'Open the door, Miss Stevens.'

'No. Go away.'

The lock rattled impatiently then the voice said, 'Nikos sent us to fetch you. Your brother is downstairs.'

Jimmy! Here! Her heart leapt for a moment and she reached for the key, then she paused. Something wasn't right. Nikos would have sent Sofia to fetch her, not some stranger. She took a deep breath then said sharply, 'Go back and tell Nikos to send my brother here. I want to hear his voice.'

She could hear another angry whispered consultation from the other side of the door then the man called back to her, 'Your brother has injured his leg. We're waiting for the doctor.'

She chewed nervously at her knuckle. Supposing they were telling the truth and Jimmy really was lying down there in pain surrounded by enemies? She put her ear flat against the door then asked, 'How . . . how did he hurt his leg? What happened to him?'

'We found him hiding up in the mountains. He tried to make a run for it but fell among some rocks.'

She straightened up. Now she knew that they were lying. Jimmy had gone nowhere near the mountains. They still hadn't found out about the missing boat. Well, she didn't need a crystal ball to guess what they were after. Desperately she looked around the room. The window was open. Could she find some way down from the balcony? Then what? Where could she go in a nightdress? Suddenly she saw the bellpush on the far wall. Would it do any good ringing for Sofia? What could the maid do? Might not the presence of somebody else at least frighten them off? Anything was worth a try. Playing for time, she called through the door, 'You . . . you'll have to wait till I get dressed.'

It didn't work. She was halfway across the room when she heard the splintering crash as the door was kicked open and she whirled round.

There were two of them: Theo, the one with the thick lips and colourless eyes, and another who could have been his younger brother. For a moment they stood drinking in the sight of her then Theo wet his lips with his tongue and said hoarsely, 'We thought you might be feeling lonely in here all by yourself. We've come to give you some company.'

'Well, you thought wrong,' she said in a tight, icy voice. 'Get out of here. The pair of you. Right now.' It was a desperate gamble but they might be scared off by a show of strength and fearlessness. Men who attacked women were usually cowards at heart.

'She's not very friendly, is she?' Theo remarked to his companion. 'We'll have to do something about that, won't we?'

She turned and made a dash for the bell but Theo was too quick for her and she screamed as he grabbed a handful of her hair and spun her around. 'Scream as loud as you like,' he sneered into her face. 'No one will hear you from here.' His breath was vile with garlic and she tried to turn her head away. He gave a signal to his companion who went behind her and wrenched her arms back. She tried to yell again but it was cut off as a hot, sweaty hand clamped itself over her mouth, making her want to gag.

There was no use pretending that she wasn't afraid any longer. She knew exactly what was on their minds and she almost choked in horror as Theo ripped her nightdress from top to bottom, leaving her exposed to his lustful gaze. For long, agonising seconds she could almost feel her skin crawling as his pale eyes roved over her with an avid rapaciousness then he began loosening the belt around his waist and snarled at her, 'Your brother struck me and left me tied up, Miss Stevens. I'm going to deal with him later but in the meantime my brother and I are going to have a little amusement with you. Nikos has already had a taste and now it's our turn.'

Sick with terror, she could feel the power leaving her legs. There was a roaring in her ears and as the man behind her suddenly let her go she slumped to the floor on her hands and knees.

'Bastards!' The voice from the doorway was an explosion of fury and, gasping for breath, she raised her head in time to see Nikos lunge at Theo. There was a tremendous crack as Nikos threw a punch which split open Theo's top lip. Clutching his mouth, Theo backed away and whined, 'For God's sake, Nikos! We're only having a little fun.'

'You think rape is funny, do you?' thundered Nikos.

'What are you worried about her for?' Theo protested angrily. 'She's just trash like her brother. That's why you went after her in the first place, isn't it? To give her——'

'Shut your filthy mouth!' Nikos glared at him and the other man, his green eyes smouldering with fury. 'You dare to call her trash! Neither one of you is fit to lick the mud off her shoes. The only trash I see here is you.'

He got down on one knee and touched her shoulder gently. 'Carrie? Can you stand?'

She tried to speak but she was still traumatised with shock and her throat was tight. Weakly she nodded her head.

'Good . . .' He put his hands under her armpits then paused and looked up at the two men who were edging their way nervously towards the door. He gave a threatening growl. 'Stay where you are. I'm not finished with you yet.'

He helped her up until she was sitting on the edge of the bed, clutching her torn nightdress around her, then turned his wrath on the two would-be rapists again. 'You've disgraced the name of Spirakis forever. I want you out of this house immediately. You'll leave as you are, in what you're wearing. Everything else you own—cars, boats, shares in the business—is now forfeit. If either of you ever comes within ten miles of this estate again I'll have you maimed for life. Now get out of my sight.'

The two men looked at each other in disbelief then Theo blustered, 'You can't do that to us! We're not going to lose everything because of that little——'

Nikos took one step towards them and that was enough to send them both scurrying from the room.

Carrie's heart was going like a trip-hammer and she was still trembling as he helped her to her feet and wrapped her tenderly in his arms. For a moment the idea of a man, even him, touching her sent an instinctive shiver of fear down her spine and she made a feeble attempt to push him away.

'No, darling,' he whispered softly. 'They've gone. You're safe now.'

Slowly, like an ebbing tide, her fear receded and his arms, which had seemed to imprison her, now became a protective barrier against the evils of the world. His hand gently stroked her hair, calming and soothing her further, and she buried her face in his chest, drawing strength from the rock-steady beat of his heart. In a muffled voice she said brokenly, 'They were going to...to...' She gulped. 'You got here just in time. How...how did you...?'

'Sofia warned me,' he said quietly. 'She heard them talking and saw them making their way here.'

'Thank God for Sofia,' she said fervently. 'I...I told them to go away but they smashed the door down.'

'I think I've let them off too lightly,' he growled darkly. 'I've a good mind to——'

'No, Nikos.' She had a vision of him cheerfully strangling them. 'Don't get yourself into trouble over them. They...they're not worth it.'

He sighed with regret. 'I suppose you have a point. They're nothing but scum.' He stroked her hair again. 'Anyway, you're safe now and that's all I care about. Try to forget it.'

Another involuntary shiver went through her. That was easy to say but she didn't think she'd forget this night as long as she lived. Things like that always happened to other people. You heard about it and felt sorry for them but you never imagined that it might be your turn one night.

Suddenly Sofia was standing in the doorway wrapped in a dressing-gown, her face pale with concern as she stared at Carrie. 'Is there anything I can do, Mr Spirakis?'

Nikos nodded at her gratefully. 'Yes, Sofia. Fetch some brandy and warm milk for Carrie. When you've done that go and prepare another room for her. A room with a spare bed for yourself, because I want you to spend the rest of the night with her.'

When the maid had gone off to carry out his orders he tilted Carrie's chin up and kissed her tenderly on the mouth then whispered, 'I let you down, darling. I guaranteed your safety in this house and this happened. Will you ever forgive me?'

She swallowed painfully and looked up into his eyes. 'Nikos...that's twice you've called me "darling". Is it just a word to you or do you really mean it?'

He kissed her again as if that were the answer to everything, but it wasn't. Love was for fools. Those words of his were still scorched across her heart. And Nikos Spirakis was no fool.

CHAPTER NINE

THE sun was streaming through the open window when Carrie was gently roused from her sleep and she struggled up, blinking. Sofia was there with a cup of hot coffee in her hand and a look of worried concern on her face. 'Good morning, Carrie. How do you feel? Nikos wants to know if you slept well. I told him yes but I don't think he believes me.'

As Carrie reached for the coffee the events of the previous night rushed through her mind with sickening clarity. The memory of those pale eyes devouring her body... the smell of his breath... the hot, sweaty hand over her mouth... then the comfort of Nikos's arms around her. By any law of nature she shouldn't have slept a wink after an experience like that but in truth she could remember very little after drinking the warm milk and brandy.

'Tell him I'm all right,' she muttered.

Sofia smiled with relief. 'Good. You can tell him yourself once things are calmer downstairs.'

Carrie sipped gratefully at the coffee then saw from the look on Sofia's face that the girl was at bursting point with news. Wondering if it possibly could have anything to do with news about her brother, she asked quickly, 'What's going on?'

Sofia glanced nervously at the door then sat down on the edge of the bed and said, 'Nikos has found out about the stolen boat. They only discovered that it was gone first thing this morning. Everyone is keeping well out of his way. They're all incompetent fools according to him. Even his own uncle. He's in a vile temper and after what he did to his two cousins they're all terrified in case he does the same to them.'

Carrie gave a despondent sigh. 'So everyone knows what happened to me last night?'

The maid shrugged regretfully. 'There are very few secrets in a place like this.'

'So that means they'll all be talking behind my back when I go down. Having a bloody good laugh, I suppose.'

'No... not at all,' Sofia assured her positively. 'Don't think that. All the staff are glad to see the last of those two pigs. They know that Nikos must think very highly of you to do what he did so from now on you're going to be very popular around here.'

'I don't intend to be around here any longer than I can help,' Carrie said wryly. She wondered what her chances of stealing a boat were now. Pretty remote, she thought. She'd just have to think of something else. Something equally desperate.

'I've washed and ironed the clothes you arrived in,' Sofia said cheerfully. 'I'll go downstairs and fetch them while you have a shower.'

'Yes...' muttered Carrie, her thoughts a million miles away and her blue eyes hard with determination. 'Thanks, Sofia. That was very good of you.'

Nikos was seated outside on the veranda having a light breakfast of scrambled eggs when she was led into his presence. He gestured at the seat opposite. 'Good morning, Carrie. Please sit down and join me. Are you hungry?'

'Thanks. The egg looks nice. I'll have some of that.' He didn't look too bad himself, she admitted grudgingly: very cool and unruffled and more devastatingly handsome than ever. How did he manage it at this time in the morning? Anyway, from what Sofia had told her she'd expected to find him biting lumps out of the furniture.

He gestured to the servant hovering near by then he grinned at her. 'That's good. I was afraid that after what you went through last night you might not be——'

'I'd rather forget about last night, if it's all the same to you. It's today I'm interested in.' She poured herself a glass of orange juice from the jug. 'Sofia told me that one of your boats is missing. I suppose my brother is getting the blame for that as well. Not content with stealing your sister, he's also taken one of your boats.' She smiled sarcastically. 'I never realised that Jimmy was such a desperado.'

'He's the obvious suspect,' Nikos said, ignoring her acidic tone. 'Even you must agree to that.'

She gave an offhand shrug. 'Too obvious perhaps. Couldn't it have been a couple of drunken tourists? Local kids? Vandals?'

'People like that would never get within a mile of this property,' he said dismissively. He stared at her and she grew uncomfortable under that shrewd and penetrating examination. She suspected that he wasn't at all fooled by her attempt to confuse and cloud the issue. She was simply playing for time—trying to gain Jimmy and Helen a breathing space and the opportunity to get married before he caught up with them. There were no facilities or authorities on Kati's island to perform a ceremony. They would simply have to lie low until the situation had cooled. She was only guessing, of course. For all she knew they might already be married but she doubted if that would deter a man like Nikos. She'd already seen him in action and he would undoubtedly just grab his sister by the scruff of the neck and drag her home kicking and screaming.

The food arrived and she heaved a mental sigh of relief as the tension was broken. Dammit, she had enough problems of her own to worry about! At least Helen hadn't been forced into pregnancy. She and Jimmy were in love with each other and they were free and they were old enough to look after themselves.

Nikos drank his coffee without once allowing his eyes to leave her face then he made his pronouncement. 'I'm going to proceed on the assumption that they did steal the boat.'

She pounced on the word immediately. 'They? Did you say "they" stole the boat? Then you've made up your mind that Helen helped him after all?'

He gave her a faint, ironic smile then swivelled his chair so that he was gazing out over the harbour towards the open sea. Watching his profile, dark against the bright sky, she felt once more that strange, self-destructive attraction. Last night his arms had been a refuge... a haven of safety and love. He'd been so gentle... so tender. Yet looking at him now she knew that it had been an illusion. Only the wishful thinking of a foolish idealist.

'Where do you think he's gone, Carrie?' he asked abruptly, his voice cutting into her thoughts like a cold steel blade.

Her eyes widened in innocence. 'How on earth would I know? I mean, if you count every little piece of scrub-covered rock out there, there must be at least two thousand islands——'

'Three thousand,' he corrected her.

She spread her hands helplessly. 'There you are, then. If I were you I'd give up. You'll never find them now.'

'Hmm...' He rubbed his temple thoughtfully with his forefinger. 'You may be right. In that case there's nothing to do but wait here until he arrives on his white charger to rescue you from my evil clutches.' The devil leered at her again from behind those green eyes.

'That might be long enough,' she said with a show of indifference. 'I dare say he's got enough on his mind right now without worrying about me.'

'I hope you're right, Carrie,' he taunted with quiet relish. 'The longer he puts it off the better as far as I'm concerned. I've already given orders for the villa to be made ready for us. From now on I'll be the one keeping watch over you during the nights.'

Her cheeks flushed, not so much at his remark but at her own stupidity for allowing him another opening—another chance to remind her of her real-life situation. Or was this his oblique way of making her an offer? She turned the possibility over in her mind. He had a pretty good idea that she knew where Jimmy would make for. Was he now trying to hint that if she told him where to find his sister he'd let her go free? A trade-off? Her freedom for help in finding his sister? In other words more moral blackmail.

She changed the subject quickly. 'Sofia is worried about losing her job. She thinks that because Helen is no longer here there's no work for her to do.'

Nikos gazed out to sea again then said, 'She helped your brother and Helen to escape, didn't she?'

She prevaricated yet again, getting used to it by now and not liking herself much in the process. 'That's something you'd better ask her yourself. It...it doesn't seem likely, does it?'

He snorted. 'Of course she did. Helen always confided in her. They were as friendly as two people ever could be.'

'So you're going to sack her as a punishment, I suppose?' She put as much contempt as she could into her voice. 'You're going to deprive her of her living because of a mere suspicion.'

He rubbed at his temple again as if he had a headache and she wasn't making it any better. 'Don't be ridiculous. I've no intention of sacking her. At least she has proved her loyalty. Misplaced, perhaps, but still a factor in her favour. She was also intelligent enough to realise what my cousins were up to last night and her presence of mind in warning me put paid to their intentions. If I had a few more people as reliable as her around here I'd be a happier man.'

'Oh...' she said in a small voice, the wind taken right out of her sails. 'She...she'll be glad to hear it.'

He eyed her with cold amusement. 'I'm sorry if I've fallen short of your expectations. I'll try to be more stony-hearted in future.'

She finished her meal in an embarrassed silence then he got to his feet and looked down at her. 'I was afraid you'd be feeling too ill used and out of sorts this morning but you've obviously recovered from your ordeal. I'm quite sure you're up to it.'

She rose and frowned at him suspiciously. 'Up to what?'

'A guided tour around the estate.'

She shook her head. 'No. Thanks all the same but I'd rather just hang around here.' A tour round the estate with him would mean being on their own together and she knew what the probable outcome of that would be.

He got that hard glint in his eye again as he reached firmly for her arm. 'I'm rather proud of what we've accomplished here, Carrie. You wouldn't want to hurt my feelings, would you?'

Oh, well, why hadn't he said so at first? The last thing she wanted to do was to hurt the poor, sensitive soul's feelings. He might go into a huff and stop talking to her altogether.

Ten minutes later she was sitting beside him in an open-topped Land Rover heading up into the hills behind the house. They wound their way through miles of olive groves and orchards, higher and higher until the tarmac road gave way to a rough boulder-strewn track. Finally they stopped and he helped her out.

The breeze tangled her long blonde hair and she had to keep sweeping it away from her eyes as she gazed at the panorama spread beneath them. It was only from up here that you could grasp the enormous size of the estate. Far below them, like something from toytown, was the white mansion, beyond that the harbour and beyond that the sparkling blue sea reflecting the mid-morning sun. She looked along the coastline to the north and south and he answered her unspoken question casually. 'Fifty kilometres either way. It's all Spirakis land.'

He pointed at the house and now there was a quiet pride in his voice. 'My great-grandfather started it all. He was a young man, newly married, when he built a wooden shack down there. He and his wife worked from dawn to dusk. They grew olives, built a press and sold the oil. Then he bought a boat and fished during the winter. They raised a family and worked hard and never owed a drachma in their life to anyone. They lived by the sweat of their brow. Their son carried on after they had died. Then his son, who was my father. Now our olive oil is sold all over Europe and that one little fishing boat has grown to a fleet of cargo ships and luxury cruisers.'

'I'm impressed,' she said. 'It's quite an achievement in only three generations.'

'More than just an achievement, Carrie,' he said quietly. 'It's the end result of a man's vision and hard work.' He paused and took one last look at the scene below. 'Perhaps now you can understand what it means to be a Spirakis. Not just the pride in the name but the legacy and the heavy burden I have to carry.'

She looked at him in stony silence then said bitterly, 'Are you asking for sympathy? From me of all people!'

His face hardened a little. 'Not sympathy. I ask that from no one. But I had hoped for understanding.'

Tearing her eyes from him, she looked at the scene below once more. His empire. His responsibility. His so-called heavy burden. Finally she turned to him and said quietly, 'All my father left to my brother and me was a clapped-out old fishing boat and a lot of poor but genuine friends. I think we got a better bargain than you did.'

Something flashed in his eyes and a shadow fleetingly crossed his already dark features. It wasn't pain or anger but something deeper. It was almost as if she'd brushed against a raw nerve. For a long moment they looked at each other in a challenging silence then he said quietly, 'I want to make love to you, Carrie. Here. Now.'

She'd had an idea that this was going to happen but the directness and suddenness still came as a shock and she managed a smile of scorn. 'You're still determined to make me pregnant, then? Still intent on doing your duty?'

'No,' he said softly. 'Neither of those reasons.'

The rushing and pounding noise was back in her ears and she had trouble getting her tongue to work. 'Look, I've already told you that . . . that——'

'I don't care what you told me.' Suddenly he moved and she found herself swept up and cradled in his arms.

She beat none too emphatically at his chest with her fists and gasped, 'Put me down! I warn you, Nikos! I'm not going to let you——'

His mouth covered hers, cutting off her protest briefly, then he said, 'Put your arms around my neck and stop arguing.'

He began walking further up the hill, his steps sure and effortless as if she weighed nothing. She took his advice and decided to hang on.

They'd only climbed about twenty metres when the ground levelled out suddenly and he put her down and began leading her by the hand towards a dilapidated stone-built cottage. Dry-mouthed and with pounding heart, she knew that it was now too late to run away and she watched in apprehension as he produced a key and opened the weathered wooden door.

From outside the place had seemed like a ruin but once inside she saw how wrong she'd been. The whole place was panelled in warm yellow pine. A deep-pile carpet covered the floor. Bookshelves lined one wall along with a stereo system and TV set. There was no bed in the one solitary room, only a long, wide divan covered in fleecy sheepskin.

He studied the expression on her face for a moment then said, 'Everyone needs a place of their own now and again. Somewhere away from the pressures of the world. This is mine.'

'It...it's very nice,' she murmured. 'I usually just put my head under the blanket.'

He smiled drily. 'That's one of the things I like about you, Carrie. That weird English sense of humour.'

'It's a national characteristic,' she muttered. 'We always face our darkest hour with a merry quip on our lips. I thought everyone knew that.'

He reached out and pulled her closer, inexorably closer, until she could feel herself once more drowning in the depths of those hungry eyes.

'Your darkest hour was last night until I came to your rescue,' he reminded her quietly. 'Or have you forgotten so soon?'

She swallowed painfully. 'I almost had. But thanks for reminding me. I suppose you feel that you're entitled to your reward now. Is that it?'

Their bodies were pressed tightly together now and she could feel the hard manifestation of his own desire. His mouth slowly descended again and her lips parted. Now his tongue...and his hands...

Her legs were starting to go and that intolerable ache was back in her loins.

He took his mouth from hers and gently nibbled at the lobe of her ear then whispered, 'Please don't insult me, Carrie. I want no reward for acting as any decent man would. What I want now is for you to give yourself freely. No threats. No promises. No strings attached.'

Her voice trembled with a half-hearted defiance, 'Why... why should I?'

'Because I want you and you want me,' he urged. 'What more genuine reason could there be?'

Her eyes were now glassy with hot, aching desire and once again she marvelled at the power this man had to provoke such an irresistible craving in her own body yet, at the same time, an even stronger compulsion to please and satisfy him.

There was no emotional reward in it for her, merely the sheer physical pleasure. They'd have sex and that would be that until the next time. She wanted more, as any woman would, but she was willingly prepared to settle for what was on offer. So what did that make her? A loose woman? A harlot? Or just an ordinary woman coping with her own feminine frailty in a pressure-cooker situation? Nikos embodied all that was best and all that was worst in the male of the species. He was a breathtakingly satisfying sexual partner but there was never any likelihood of him confusing the act of sex with a commitment of love.

The words bubbled up from her throat, 'Damn you, Nikos! You... you know the answer. I... I can't help wanting you.'

His hands slipped beneath her T-shirt and his fingers deftly undid the bra. 'Good...' he whispered. 'Those are the words I wanted to hear.'

He undressed her with an exquisite, leisurely indulgence, removing each article of her clothing to a nerve-throbbing accompaniment of kisses on each piece of newly exposed flesh. When her briefs were lowered his kisses became deeper and more urgent as his mouth travelled up her inner thigh until she suddenly gasped and threw her head back, quivering at this new, totally unexpected experience. Her fingers curled themselves frantically in his dark hair and she stifled a cry. When she was almost at the edge of total and abandoned frenzy he took his mouth away and stood up. Gently he lifted her and carried her over to the divan and she lay on her back, gazing up at him beneath lids heavy and half-closed with pulsating anticipation as he slowly undressed.

Finally, he was naked and he stood over her, his dark skin glistening like silk. Her hot, sultry gaze travelled upwards past the corded muscles of his powerful thighs to the gorged tumescence of his manhood, taut and proud. Above that his stomach, hard and flat, then the deep chest and broad shoulders. He looked like some darkly magnificent creation of the gods sent to pander to her most shameful and unspoken desires.

As he leaned over her she reached for him, her arms wide and her fingers outstretched like some supplicant begging for relief. Carefully he eased his dark, lithe body beside her and she eagerly sought his mouth with her own. His right hand clasped her bottom, pulling her closer, and she felt the proud and rampant flesh of his sexuality against her thigh.

Her breasts were pressed against his chest, her nipples swollen and aching. The smell and the taste of him were inflaming her senses to a white incandescence and she drew one knee up and hooked her left leg over his and began sliding her calf up and down his thigh.

A low, almost animal growl of approval came from his throat and he took his mouth from hers to murmur, 'I want you, Carrie!'

She felt a mounting frustration as he continued to tease her with his mouth and tongue instead of pinning her down and claiming possession. And then, blindingly, it came to her what he wanted. For a moment the last shreds of her natural modesty were shocked at the idea then her libido broke free and at the gentle urging of his hand she squirmed her body until she was sitting astride him, her knees level with his waist. He reached up for her shoulders and pulled her upper body forward until her palms were resting either side of him on the divan, and now her breasts, like ripe fruit ready to fall, were only inches above his face. He took one of her nipples in his mouth and feasted hard in an erotic indulgence that sent her into a fit of feverish panting. His hands moulded themselves around her slim waist and down over her hips then gently he began to lift her. As his mouth released her breast she straightened up and shivered with anticipation.

Her actions now owed nothing to experience but were dictated by urgency and instinct. As he slowly lowered her she reached down between her legs to guide him in. The slow, lubricous entry sent waves of molten fire through her loins and tiny moans of ecstatic pleasure escaped her half-parted and swollen lips. He was reaching upwards now, rubbing and teasing each of her nipples between his fingers and thumbs.

Utterly lost now in an ocean of sensuality, she began to ride the waves of her own passion. Beneath her he suddenly groaned in pleasure and as his warm essence flooded into her her muscles contracted. She arched her spine and threw her head back and cried out in ecstastic disbelief as the spasms continued. Gasping and wide-eyed, she realised that he still hadn't finished as his powerful hands held her still and his hips rose, thrusting himself ever deeper and faster.

Oh, God! she thought with awestruck wonder. She was . . . she was going to . . . yet again!

When it was finally over she literally collapsed, still astride him but with her damp forehead leaning on his chest. Gently he tilted her face upwards and kissed her mouth with a lingering tenderness.

At last she put her hands on his chest and straightened up. 'I'm exhausted. I feel as if I've just run a marathon.'

He looked up at her with a smile of lazy contentment on his face and murmured, 'You're good at that. Exceptionally good.'

Her passion was spent now. No doubt her old friends guilt and self-recrimination would soon pay her a visit but at the moment she could still live with herself. 'What does "exceptionally good" mean?' she asked. 'Better than your other women?'

'Much, much better,' he drawled. 'Of all the hundreds I've known you are without doubt the most passionate.'

She saw the gleam of dark humour in his eyes and suddenly all the magic was gone. She was just a fool and he was having a good laugh at her expense. She eased herself off him and swung her legs to the floor.

His hand reached out and gripped her arm. 'Where do you think you're going?'

'To get dressed.' She looked at him blandly. 'We both got what we wanted, didn't we? And now it's over.

He rolled on to his side and propped himself up on one elbow. 'Stay here. We've got to talk.'

She bit her lip. 'If it's about my brother and your sister, forget it. I've got nothing else to say about them.' He ran his fingers suggestively up and down her thigh and she lifted his hand firmly and put it away. 'Don't start that again.'

He raised a quizzical eyebrow and managed to look hurt. 'Why? I thought you were in love with me?'

'Don't be...don't be ridiculous.' She tried to pull her arm free but his grip was too tight and she looked at him resentfully. 'You're going to bruise my arm.'

'Then admit that you're in love with me,' he demanded.

'You'll break my arm if I don't?' she scoffed. 'What will that prove?'

He released her then said softly, 'All right Carrie. Now admit it.'

Her heart came into her mouth and she looked away, unable to stand the scrutiny of his eyes. 'You...you're mad,' she muttered. 'I...I might have said that I liked you once. But that was in one of my weaker moments. Before I really got to know you.' How could she lie like this? she thought in anguish. She really did love the arrogant, chauvinistic, autocratic devil but wild horses wouldn't drag that admission from her mouth. He would just start ridiculing her again and tell her that love was for stupid idealists like her.

Suddenly he reached up and gripped her jaw between his fingers and thumb and squeezed gently until her lips formed a perfect O. 'You have the most wonderful mouth in the world,' he mused. 'Why do you spoil it by filling it with lies when the truth is so obvious in a hundred other ways?'

She gulped and said, 'Uhh uhss?' Pulling his hand away, she tried again. 'It is?'

'Of course it is. You've just proved it.'

Colour touched her cheeks. 'Look . . . I'd like to put my clothes on now if you don't mind.'

'I do mind,' he said with a taunting smile. 'I like looking at you the way you are.'

The colour stayed in her cheeks and she said stiffly, 'That may well be. But I find it embarrassing.'

'You didn't when we were aboard the *Miranda*.'

'That was different.'

He gave a low, throaty chuckle. 'It's just a state of mind, Carrie. When you think of what we were doing to each other a few minutes ago it's a bit fastidious of you to feel shy in my company.' His hand, which she'd removed from her thigh, was now tracing a delicate path between the nape of her neck and the bottom of her spine and she tried her best to ignore it because she knew that if she attempted to get up he'd just grab her again. Anyway, he was right. She was acting like a schoolgirl instead of a mature woman and by God hadn't he seen to it that she'd matured? He probably had a black belt in maturing young women. She looked down at him lying there like some dark satyr from

Greek mythology. He'd be asking her to feed him grapes in a minute, she thought drily.

'Do you know why I brought you up here, Carrie?' he asked her quietly.

'Yes, I've got a pretty good idea,' she muttered, eyeing her clothes strewn about the floor.

'Do you think that it was just to have sex?' he demanded.

She could feel her eyes growing hot. 'No. I was forgetting. You wanted to show me your empire, didn't you? You wanted me to understand about your "duty" and the heavy burden you had to bear.'

He nodded. 'That's right. I wanted you to know why a Spirakis couldn't afford to fall in love.'

'Yes,' she said tiredly. 'Please don't go into it all again, Nikos. I'm sick of hearing about it. Anyway I'm sure there are plenty of eminently suitable young ladies from good families who are only too willing to enhance your good name and share your burdens.'

'Yet in spite of knowing that you still agreed to make love with me?'

'Did I have any option?' she asked angrily.

'You could have refused,' he pointed out calmly. 'You were under no threat. No pressure. No strings. Remember? Now I know that I've given you every reason in the world to hate and despise me and yet you still gave yourself to me freely. I want to know why.'

Her blue eyes took on the hard glint of sapphire and she clenched her fists in frustration. He had no right to subject her to this kind of interrogation. He already knew the secrets of her body but that wasn't good enough for him. He wanted to invade her mind as well.

His voice came at her again, harsher and even more insistent. 'Tell me, Carrie. It's important. I've got to know.'

She held out for another few stomach-churning seconds then she snapped at him, 'All right, dammit! It's because I wanted to.' She was too quick for him as she got to her feet and reached for her briefs. 'Don't pretend that you don't know the effect you have on women. I'm no different from any of your other...conquests. Another scalp. Another notch on your belt to brag about.'

He flashed his white teeth in a grin then commented drily, 'Sex is a funny business, Carrie. It's supposed to be an act of love but in most cases it's an act of selfishness. Most people merely indulge in it for the pleasure it gives them personally. But not you. Just now you were as much concerned about pleasing me as you were about yourself. Only people in love do that.'

She picked up his trousers and threw them at him angrily. 'Will you put these on and make yourself decent? You don't know what you're talking about.'

He swung himself off the divan and dressed himself unhurriedly. When he'd finished he said, 'That's the real reason I brought you here, Carrie. To find out how you really felt about me. You can stand there denying that you love me until you're blue in the face but I know what's really in that heart of yours.'

Suddenly it was all too clear to her now and as the realisation sank home and bit deep she felt a hot flush of anger. 'I suppose you're happy now,' she mouthed at him bitterly. 'Your victory is complete. Not only have you probably made the little idiot pregnant but she's actually fallen in love with you. That's the real icing on your cake, isn't it?' A tear began to roll down her cheek and she brushed it away angrily.

His dark brows came together and he shook his head. 'You couldn't be more wrong, Carrie. If you want to know the truth I——'

'Truth!' she yelled at him. 'What the hell do you know about truth? Or decency? Or respect for other people's feelings? You may have saved me from being raped by those two cousins of yours but the reality is that there's very little difference between you and them. I'm not surprised your own sister wants nothing more to do with this family.' Another tear rolled down her cheek. 'I hope you end up married to some black-hearted bitch who makes your life a living hell.'

He sighed heavily. 'She probably will after the way I've treated her.'

'Good!' she flung at him. 'I wish her the best of luck.'

There was something in his eyes and his smile that she'd never seen before. Warmth! Not the usual mockery nor sarcasm that had seemed as much a part of his nature as the dark olive of his skin. She considered this new phenomenon and looked at him uncertainly, wondering what was going through that devilish mind now. Another way to humiliate her? No. It couldn't be. Not with a smile like that. Her confusion became deeper as he spread his arms wide and said softly, 'Come here, Carrie.'

Her throat felt dry and tight and she regarded him with deep suspicion. 'W-why?'

'Because it's where you belong.'

Her voice trembled now. 'I . . . I'm warning you, Nikos. Stop playing games with me. I've had about all I can stand.'

'This is no game, Carrie,' he assured her in a quiet voice.

She fixed her blue eyes on him, searching his face—challenging him. 'Yes, it is. I . . . I know you by now.'

He sighed in mild exasperation. 'You're going to have to learn to stop arguing with me, Carrie. In public at least. I can't have people thinking that Nikos Spirakis can't control his wife.'

Wariness crept into her eyes. She remained tight-lipped, afraid to say anything in case she made an even bigger fool of herself than she already had. It had sounded as if . . . as if . . . But that couldn't be right. She must have misunderstood him.

'What's the matter?' He frowned at her. 'Didn't you hear what I said? Or have you no wish to become Mrs Spirakis?'

There was no mistake about it now! He was actually asking her to marry him! She wet her lips nervously with her tongue. 'Why?' she asked at last. 'I mean . . . after all you've said about . . .' She ran out of words. If he told her that it was because he was feeling sorry for her or because of the child she was probably carrying . . . If he even hinted at anything like that she'd——

'Because I love you, Carrie,' he said softly.

Her heart tripped then gave a thud. 'But . . . but you said that . . . your duty . . .'

'I was wrong, Carrie. Terribly wrong. Now are you coming to my arms or do I have to come and get you?'

This wasn't happening, she told herself in a daze. It couldn't be! If she ran to his arms now the bubble would burst and she'd be met with mocking laughter. She took one hesitant step towards him and then another and then suddenly she was enfolded in his arms.

Even then she still couldn't trust the evidence of her own eyes or senses. She couldn't allow herself to believe in the impossible. She was dreaming! Yes, that was it! A bright and vivid dream. They'd made love to each other on the divan then she'd fallen asleep in his arms. Any moment now she'd wake up. And yet... It was so real. She could feel the strength of his arms... feel the steady beat of his heart in his chest... feel his warm breath against her cheek.

'You still haven't given me your answer, Carrie,' he murmured softly.

Emotion was welling up in her throat and she swallowed. 'Yes, Nikos. I'll marry you. If you're sure... I mean... truly certain that you love me.'

'Thank God,' he said fervently, and she could almost feel the huge surge of relief rushing through his body. 'After the way I've treated you I never imagined that you could find it in your heart to forgive me.'

She looked up at him, her eyes wide in joyous wonder. 'Neither did I, Nikos. But then I never imagined that a man like you could fall in love with me.'

'Oh, I'm in love with you, darling. Don't doubt that for one minute.' His voice was thick with bitter self-reproach. 'It didn't happen in a blinding flash, darling. At first it was just a... just a feeling that

I tried to ignore. And then—during the storm—the feeling turned to something stronger. Something I couldn't ignore any longer. But I couldn't allow it to happen.' He gave a harsh laugh of self-deprecation. 'I tried to explain to you . . . and even as I was spouting platitudes about my duty and the honour of my family the words were sticking in my throat. And then, last night, I saw a good example of the family honour I was so determined to uphold.'

She pressed her finger to his lips, feeling his pain, trying to soothe the ache of guilt. 'No, darling. That had nothing to do with you. You can't take the blame for those——'

He shook his head. 'No. You're wrong about that. I must blame myself. I'd never liked Theo but I deliberately closed my eyes to the kind of man he was because he was a Spirakis and family loyalty always had to come first.' He stroked her hair gently and gazed down deeply into her eyes. 'I know now how wrong I've been. I told you once that I was a realist but it took a long time for the truth finally to come home to me.'

She stood on tiptoe and kissed him tenderly. 'What truth?'

'That love is stronger than blind loyalty.' He returned her kiss then went on, 'My great-grandparents, who began all this, loved one another, and it must have been that love that sustained them through the years of hard work and deprivation. But ever since then the Spirakis family has forgotten that fundamental truth and the only thing they've been interested in is their own self-importance. Well, all that is going to change, Carrie. You and I are going to see to that.'

It was the longest speech she'd ever heard him make and she didn't need telling that it came straight from his heart. She only wished that her father were still alive to witness this. He'd readily have approved of all those sentiments and he and Nikos would have got on well together.

Her frantically beating pulse was settling down again to something just a little above normal. All her fears and misgivings had gone and in their place was a feeling of warm happiness. Only one question remained to be resolved and she ventured softly, 'What about Helen and Jimmy?'

'Ah, yes. Our pair of young runaway lovers.' His eyes grew thoughtful. 'I owe them a great debt of gratitude, Carrie. If it hadn't been for them my eyes would never have been opened to the power of love. And I'd never have met you.'

'I'm longing to meet your sister, Nikos.' She smiled at him awkwardly. 'Look . . . I think that I may have an idea . . . No. I'm pretty sure I know where they are. We could set sail from here and——'

He shook his head and grinned. 'I think we'll let them stay with Kati for a few more days and then we can fetch them back.'

'How did you know that they'd gone to Kati's island?' she asked in astonishment.

He shrugged. 'When I learnt that Jimmy had stolen a boat I asked myself where he'd head for. He'd know that we'd have people scouring the Aegean for him so it would have to be some out-of-the-way island where he'd feel secure.' He grinned and brushed her worries away with a kiss on the forehead. 'As soon as the *Miranda* is ready we'll go and tell them the good news. If they're not married by then we'll arrange a double wedding.'

'But...but the *Miranda* is ready now. We can leave right away.'

'And spoil their fun?' He raised an amused eyebrow. 'They're on a secluded little island with a lovely beach. And they're in love and have lots of lost time to make up for. If you were in their place would you welcome company?'

She gave a slightly embarrassed smile. 'I...I suppose you're right. I never thought about it that way.'

'As for the *Miranda*...' He took her by the hand and headed for the door. 'Follow me. I've got a little surprise for you.'

He led her down the hill towards the Land Rover. Reaching in, he took a pair of binoculars from the shelf under the dashboard and handed them to her. 'Look at your boat and tell me what you see.'

She focused the glasses and stared through them for a full minute before handing them back with a frown. 'There are men on the deck, Nikos. What are they doing to my boat?'

'Carrying out the orders I gave them first thing this morning.' He glanced at her sideways and grinned apologetically. 'You see, even before you agreed to marry me I was making plans. Those men down there are about to give *Miranda* a complete overhaul and refit. By the time they're finished the living accommodation will be as good as anything you'll find on our luxury cruisers.' He took the glasses from her and tossed them back in the Land

Rover then put his arms around her waist and said gravely, '*Miranda* is a grand old lady. She may have seen better days but she'll never end up on the scrap heap as long as you and I are still alive, darling. She's given us too many good memories for that.'

She smiled dreamily up into his eyes. 'Like the time you fixed her rudder and I had to wash your back?'

He pulled her closer. 'The way she battled through that storm. And the first time we made love. On deck . . . under the stars.'

'And the next morning,' she reminded him, 'when you tossed me overboard—and I was sure I would drown but you made sure that I didn't . . . in your own special way.'

They looked into each other's eyes, sharing the memories . . . the laughter . . . the danger . . . sharing love. Their lips finally met with a tenderness that said it all. After all that they'd gone through theirs was a love that simply had to last forever.

Next Month's Romances

Each month you can choose from a wide variety of romance with Mills & Boon. Below are the new titles to look out for next month, why not ask either Mills & Boon Reader Service or your Newsagent to reserve you a copy of the titles you want to buy – just tick the titles you would like and either post to Reader Service or take it to any Newsagent and ask them to order your books.

Please save me the following titles:	Please tick	✓
ENEMY WITHIN	Amanda Browning	
THE COLOUR OF MIDNIGHT	Robyn Donald	
VAMPIRE LOVER	Charlotte Lamb	
STRANGE INTIMACY	Anne Mather	
SUMMER OF THE STORM	Catherine George	
ICE AT HEART	Sophie Weston	
OUTBACK TEMPTATION	Valerie Parv	
DIVIDED BY LOVE	Kathryn Ross	
DARK SIDE OF THE ISLAND	Edwina Shore	
IN THE HEAT OF PASSION	Sara Wood	
SHADOW OF A TIGER	Jane Donnelly	
BEWARE A LOVER'S LIE	Stephanie Howard	
PASSIONATE OBSESSION	Christine Greig	
SWEET MADNESS	Sharon Kendrick	
STRANGER AT THE WEDDING	Joan Mary Hart	
VALERIE	Debbie Macomber	
OBLIGATION TO LOVE	Catherine O'Connor	

If you would like to order these books in addition to your regular subscription from Mills & Boon Reader Service please send £1.90 per title to: Mills & Boon Reader Service, Freepost, P.O. Box 236, Croydon, Surrey, CR9 9EL, quote your Subscriber No:................................... (If applicable) and complete the name and address details below. Alternatively, these books are available from many local Newsagents including W H Smith, J Menzies, Martins and other paperback stockists from 10 June 1994.

Name:...

Address:...

....Post Code:.........................

To Retailer: If you would like to stock M&B books please contact your regular book/magazine wholesaler for details.

You may be mailed with offers from other reputable companies as a result of this application. If you would rather not take advantage of these opportunities please tick box ☐